ALWAYS DEAD

ALWAYS DEAD

WELCOME TO DEAD HOUSE™ BOOK TWO

M.L. BULLOCK

DISRUPTIVE IMAGINATION

Copyright © 2020 Monica L. Bullock
Cover by Fantasy Book Design
Cover copyright © LMBPN Publishing

LMBPN Publishing
PMB 196, 2540 South Maryland Pkwy
Las Vegas, NV 89109

First US Edition May, 2020
eBook ISBN: 978-1-64202-930-7
Print ISBN: 978-1-64202-931-4

This book is for you, Kevin. You are a true plot master and a good friend. Thank you for allowing me to spend half my life writing. I like the other half too.

THE ALWAYS DEAD TEAM

Thanks to our Beta Team:
Jim Caplan, John Ashmore, Kelly O'Donnell, Rachel Beckford, Mary Morris, Larry Omans

Thanks to the JIT Readers

Micky Cocker
Veronica Stephan-Miller
Debi Sateren
Deb Mader
Diane L. Smith
Kerry Mortimer
Angel LaVey

If I've missed anyone, please let me know!

Editor
Lynne Stiegler

TAMARA

I opened the dryer, and a string of swear words flew out of my mouth. Joey, or at least a part of him, had his head and shoulders hunkered inside the appliance.

"Joey? What the hell? Are you trying to scare me to death?" I didn't mean to sound angry, but his hiding in unexpected places was becoming a problem. I didn't mind living with a ghost, but enough with the funhouse surprises. I didn't understand Joey's weird obsession with electrical appliances.

"Are you trying to kill yourself again? We've been through this. It's not possible. You're already dead."

He scowled at me. "You don't have to be rude, Tamara. What a potty mouth. Keep your voice down. I don't want the 'visitor,'" he whispered as he made air quotes, "to know I'm in here. Close the door and go away." I shook my head and waved my hand in frustration.

"No. I'm not going anywhere. Who are you talking about? Chloe isn't here, remember? She went to spend the night with Lynn. Unless you're saying there's another ghost in the house."

He didn't say anything but put his finger to his lips.

"I've got laundry to do so if you wouldn't mind hiding somewhere else?"

"Quiet, loudmouth! Are you telling me you haven't seen that horrible wretch of a ghost? Way to go, Miss Paranormal Investigator. She's been hanging around your office. It's that book you're writing. I thought it was Chloe and her woo-woo crap but it's you. Your writing is attracting activity, Tamara. I'm sure of it!"

I shook my head at the suggestion that somehow I was the cause of his latest freak out. "Listen, I'm down to no underwear, so if you wouldn't mind?"

Joey faded a little, which worried me a bit. My best friend was easy to read. When he was happy and everything was going okay, he was luminous; he practically glowed. When Joey was stressed or worried or frustrated, and it was hard to believe the dead can be any of those things, he faded in and out and went translucent. At the moment, I could barely see him. He moaned as if he were in pain. This was disturbing. Something was up for sure.

"What's going on with you? Where did you see her?" I asked, concerned his fear appeared to be climbing. Despite the fact he was a ghost and enjoyed binge-watching paranormal investigation shows, Joey did not like the idea of other spirits being anywhere around him. He was more afraid of them than Chloe and me.

He whispered up at me, "I wouldn't have to hide in places like this if you let me have my own room. This is on you, Tamara."

I drew back, feeling exasperated. So that's what this was about? Hiding in the dryer was just a ploy to get me to change my mind about room renovations. "We've talked about this, Joey. I don't have the money to renovate a room right now. Pick an empty bedroom and hang out in it. The most I can offer you is a box to hide in. There's no money in the budget for a bedroom set and all the accessories on your wish list. Maybe later when the legal stuff with Chloe is worked out."

"That's bull. You have the money. You just got a book deal."

Rolling my eyes at his assertion, I tossed a dryer sheet in on him. "No, I didn't. I haven't heard a thing yet. Do you know something I don't?"

He stuck his tongue out at me. "I know a lot but whatever. Nice to know I'm a priority, best friend. Bestie. BFF."

"Come on. Give me a break. Is there really a ghost in here right now, Joey? Or did you freak yourself out watching that Amityville Horror marathon? Are you actually being threatened or are you just being extra?"

He crossed his arms and turned his face away from me. Feeling extra myself, extra aggravated, I dumped my wet clothing on top of him as he moaned again. "Disgusting, Tamara!" I slammed the dryer door and flipped the switch.

"Those panties are clean, Joey! If you don't want to talk, you can hang out with my underwear. Otherwise, I'm going to the mailbox." I paused as Joey mumbled something, but since the dryer door was closed and in full operation, I couldn't make out what he was saying. "You'll need to come out of there if you want to talk to me." I waited for him to manifest but he didn't appear. "Be a stubborn ass then."

With a sigh, I slid my flip-flops on to make the trek to the mailbox. I noticed the entryway chandelier wobbled a little, and I studied the movement for a moment. Usually it only happened when Chloe had her music up loud or she and Lynn were working on some dance or God knows what else. There wasn't a soul up there right now, so I had no explanation for it.

Nothing else appeared to be moving around. I thought maybe I should break out the EMF detector, just in case.

Once the chandelier stopped wobbling, I left the house and made the walk to the mailbox which was located at the end of the long driveway. It was a hot afternoon as it always seemed to be in Crystal Springs, Louisiana. Falls and winters weren't very cool here from what I experienced. It certainly didn't feel like fall.

It was November, and the leaves were crunching beneath my flip-flops. The sky was overcast, and I caught myself looking back at the Ridaught Plantation a few times as I made my way. I don't know what I expected to see in those windows—perhaps a malevolent face staring down at me from the attic or a second-floor window, a clue as to what was beginning to manifest. Joey was definitely worked up, and I had been having plenty of dreams.

Young guy in a hot car and the feeling of being choked. So weird. Before coming here, I wasn't one to dream much. That had certainly changed.

In my limited experience at the Dead House, the name locals gave the Ridaught Plantation, those top floors were the most haunted. Unless you included Joey's activities as hauntings, which I did not. Most of the time, Joey roamed all over the house, except for Chloe's room. That space was off-limits to everyone unless you wanted to deal with an angry teenager. I couldn't figure out why he'd suddenly decided he wanted his own room.

With my hand shielding my eyes against the setting sun, I studied the house again. There was nothing there. No one was watching, and there was nothing to account for the wobbling chandelier. At least there were no ghostly figures or shadow people leering at me. For all I knew, Joey might be having a bit of fun at my expense. He was a prankster at times, but never anything malicious.

I wasn't surprised to see my mailbox stuffed with envelopes. There were the usual circulars and unwanted junk mail, and even a letter addressed to my neighbor. Shoot. I'd have to take it to her. The last thing I wanted to do was visit Linda Blabbermouth, as Joey unaffectionately called the nosy neighbor, but I'd have to. Just not right this second. What was up with the mail lady recently? This was the second time this week.

I sorted through a few more envelopes and then paused. I'd received a letter from Bright House Publishing. I submitted my book to them recently, too recently for this to be a good letter. God, please don't let this be another rejection letter.

Have a little faith, Tamara. Thirteen was always your lucky number. The thirteenth was the charm, remember?

It was strange that my internal voice of encouragement always sounded like my late best friend, Tina Louise. Shoving the rest of the envelopes under an arm, I tore the letter open and scanned the subject line for the dreaded word REJECTION. To my surprise, I didn't see it.

We are happy to inform you that your book The Ghost of Crystal Springs *has been accepted for publication. Please contact us at your earliest convenience at...*

I shrieked in surprise. Like a kid holding an ice cream, I jumped up and down and looked around me for someone to share my good news with. There were no neighbors out, so I had no one to explain my joy to. Surprisingly, Linda's car wasn't there either.

Wait, Joey knew about this! He knew this was going to happen. Well, he would just have to come out of the dryer because this was cause for celebration.

I raced back to the house, my flip-flops flapping on the leaves as I ran. It was never a good idea to run in flip-flops, but this was a special occasion. As I swung the door open, I screamed for Joey. "Joey! Come out of the dryer! You have to see this!"

I dropped the remainder of the mail on the foyer table and unfolded the letter completely so I could take it all in. Yes, I had read it correctly.

Bright House Publishing wanted my book!

"Joey! I'm about to be a published author! Come see the letter! It's time to celebrate!"

I could barely breathe, I was so happy, but my joy was short-lived.

My calls for Joey echoed back to me, and the house felt extraordinarily empty. Since it was the last place I had seen Joey, I went back to the dryer, hoping he might still be hanging out there. He wasn't, or if he was, I sure couldn't see him. He was nowhere to be found, not in the dryer nor the washing machine. I also checked the oven and refrigerator, just in case.

I read the letter again. Could this be right? It had to be. I had the letter to prove it.

"Joey, come out, come out, wherever you are. Big news! You called it, Joey! I got a deal!"

I heard not a sound.

As I walked around the house, the air felt kind of odd and unsettled.

Kind of crackly and very still, the air hung like a blanket. Not humid exactly, more like a kind of smothering. It reminded me of times when you walked in the woods and everything got quiet because there was a predator, like a coyote or a bobcat. I had experienced such moments when I'd been on past paranormal investigations in remote locations.

Like the Campbell Cabin in Rhode Island. That place had been a total creep-fest. That was the night Tina Louise and I caught glowing orbs on camera and heard groans.

That's exactly what was happening here. It was time to take the bull by the horns and see for myself. Where had I put my EMF detector?

Joey knew about the letter and was probably right about the new ghost at the Ridaught Plantation. If there was a new haunting, I wanted to know about it now. Better to be proactive.

My joyous mood took a nosedive as I surveyed my surroundings. I piled all the letters on the nearest table and focused on the house. I should hear something, but there wasn't a sound.

Not the usual low hum from the air conditioning vents,

no running refrigerator, nothing at all. It was as if I were standing inside a vacuum, and all the noise had been sucked away. I whispered Joey's name, and I couldn't even hear my own voice.

Well, that was different.

I couldn't hear a thing—not Joey's awful singing or laughing or even him clattering down the hall in my heels.

I was suddenly awash with heavy emotions, and they weren't mine. I'd been kind of lonely lately, but I had not experienced anything quite like this...whatever it was. I gripped the edge of the table as I tried to fight back against whoever was forcing me to experience this.

"I'm not a medium," I said to whoever might be listening. "Stop doing that. I don't like it." It felt like I had been dropped into a vat of heavy, sad molasses. Then a blast of heat whooshed past my face and the feeling was gone.

The hairs on my arms stood up, and I knew without a shadow of a doubt, despite my attempts at mocking Joey and belittling his fears, we had a new resident at Dead House. The thick weird feeling began to let up, and I managed to get myself together.

"Hello? Whoever you are, I felt what you did to me, and I don't like it. My name is Tamara, and this is my home. If you want to talk to me, I'm listening, but we have rules here." I waited for a response. Not a peep. "No touching anyone. No hurting anyone. You'll have to find a way to tell me what you need but leave Joey alone. He's off-limits. Okay? You can't harm him. Hello?"

I thought about what Joey said earlier about my writing adding fuel to the fire here at the Dead House. Was I some sort of paperback medium, and my new book had attracted unwanted paranormal attention?

I had classified my book as fiction, not non-fiction, and not a true memoir of any sort. My latest book had been inspired by a dream I had, one I'd had several times. Surely, my fiction had nothing to do with the potential paranormal presence attempting to make itself known here at the Ridaught Plantation. Whatever the reason, I had to investigate.

I went to my room and found my EMF detector and the digital recorder. I walked back to the front room and tried a few other conversation starters with the invisible entity. The EMF spiked up to the red before it fell back to green. It only lasted a few seconds, but that was it. No one wanted to talk. This new entity wasn't ready to reveal herself yet.

Just as sure as the sun came up in the morning, I knew it would manifest sooner rather than later. That was the thing I liked the least about paranormal investigation, the unhappy surprises.

Like being startled or walking into the intangible and feeling that weird spider web feeling all over your body, but hey, what was a girl going to do? I was up for the job. I had this. Now I had to figure out how to tell Chloe. Maybe she already knew. The teenager was a strong, natural medium. Unfortunately, she was in one of those "I don't want to talk to Aunt Tamara" moods.

Oh, well. I could handle this.

All by myself.

2

TAMARA

After another thirty minutes of taking readings and getting no responses, I went into the kitchen to heat up a can of soup for supper. As I stirred the contents, I listened to the recordings at full volume.

Not a peep. Not a word or a sound that would lead me to believe anyone or anything had responded. I debated what next. I could try some Rem Pods, or turn off the lights and walk around with the IR camera. I had batteries for all of them.

I secretly hoped Chloe would change her mind and come home tonight. Maybe I could call her and ask her to bring me a pizza. I couldn't leave, but I wasn't looking forward to this soup.

Too bad, Tamara. Soup. It's what's for dinner. If you're lucky, you may have a few crackers to go with it.

I continued to stir the chicken-flavored concoction and then retrieved a bowl and spoon from the cabinet. I could not call Chloe and pull her away from her fun. That would be very lame of me, and I was lame enough already, according to her. I'd share the good news with Chloe when she came home tomorrow afternoon. And of course, tell her about the new ghost.

This whole being-a-mom thing was beyond me. Tina Louise, Chloe's late mother, had been my best friend, yet I felt as if I knew nothing about her. For a long time, I didn't even know she had a kid, much less a family home or such a remarkable family lineage.

Why would you keep all this a secret from Chloe and me? Why would you do that, Tina Louise?

Tina Louise was as much a mystery to me now as she was back in the day when we were working together. Those had been good times, though. When we weren't chasing ghosts on paranormal ghost tours, we spent our time together being creative, critiquing one another on our dance arrangements and choreography.

The two of us had collaborated on some of the East Coast's most popular burlesque shows. She'd been kind from day one but ruthless when it came to business. Tina Louise was one of the few dancers I knew who had the moxie to negotiate her own contracts with some of the shadiest club owners you'd ever want to meet. She taught me so much, but she left us too quickly.

I learned a lot from the redheaded siren.

Her passing had been only a few months ago, but it felt like a lifetime. TL had gone too soon, way too soon.

The house remained quiet, but at least the strange molasses feeling did not return. The entity did not try again to project her emotions on me. I had not enjoyed that at all. Joey was hiding somewhere, or he had gone to a safe place to recover. As always, I hoped he came back safe and sound.

I couldn't imagine life without him now, although that was probably very selfish of me. I had always believed it was best for spirits to pass on and not linger in this realm after their death. But Joey? When it came to him, I selfishly hoped he would stick around for a long time.

From what I gathered, from the sparse hints he sometimes dropped, Joey visited the neighbor's house and harassed her on the regular. Maybe he was over there now tormenting Linda by slamming doors or stomping around, which was probably a better alternative than hanging out here with whoever this ghost might be.

I should have been more sympathetic when I found Joey in the dryer.

A few minutes later, I sat down alone at my wobbly kitchen table to enjoy my boring soup, along with a bottle of water and the last of my crackers. As I ate, I began plotting tonight's investigation. Rem Pods for sure. Easy-peasy.

I'd have to go to the grocery store soon, or I would be forced to eat the frozen vegetables in my freezer. I couldn't for the life of me understand why I continued buying vegetables when nobody in this house ate them. It just felt like the responsible thing to do.

The house felt emptier than usual. Too big, and too empty.

After eating about half of my soup, I threw the rest away and began setting up the Rem Pods. They were basically proximity sensors that flashed and screeched when anyone got near them.

I retrieved three of them and decided to put two in the

hallway and one in the front room. It wasn't quite dark, but I turned the lights off anyway. I used the digital recorder and tried to catch something, but nothing happened. I went at it for an hour, moving the equipment around, and trying different tactics. I even asked the ghost to respond with a yes or no answer by using a flashlight.

It was pointless. Whoever she was, she didn't want to talk to me. Eventually, I gave up and put all the equipment back in my closet. I changed my clothes and sat on the couch, hoping to lure Joey out of hiding.

"Joey, there's a new show on. Come watch it with me."

There was nothing on television. I hated the commercials, and I'd already watched everything on my DVR. I toyed with the idea of adding some details to my book outline, but my brain was mush. I read the letter from the publisher a dozen times before I went to bed. I would call the publishing house in the morning to hear more about the details of what they were offering me. The letter was kind of vague.

That was probably the case. This had to be too good to be true. Nobody hit the publishing jackpot on the first book. Then again, I had received more than my share of rejection letters. At least it felt that way. In a recent interview on *Good Morning, Louisiana*, popular author Bernadette Lewis let it drop she had been rejected nearly a hundred times before her book *Spirit of Spring* was selected by Yorktown for publication. I guess in the grand scheme of things, I'd really hit the jackpot, depending on what they offered.

Yeah, Tamara Garvey. Don't count your chickens before they hatch.

Strangely enough, it did not take me a lifetime to write my first book. I wrote it in record time. Those writing sessions had been so surreal, as if someone else had been doing the writing and I was just along for the ride.

Almost like a dang ghostwriter stood over my shoulders, whispering in my ear.

I decided to call it a day. I'd do more investigative work tomorrow after my walk. I wanted to check out a few locations around the property. I felt as if I were missing an important clue relative to my dream, something that would lead me to the true identity of the young man in my book. No doubt he'd been a resident of Crystal Springs at one time, or at least a visitor. I flicked off the light and closed the door to my office.

I brushed my teeth, kicked off my floppy slippers, and slid under the clean sheets. I was tired, and I'd done very little today. I was kind of glad Joey made himself scarce because I didn't have the energy to hang out and watch paranormal investigation shows all night as he often liked doing on the weekends. I had the DVR recording *Haunted Case Files* and a few other shows. We'd catch up on them later together.

Truth be told, it had been that strange encounter with the invisible entity which had drained me.

There was definitely a ghost in residence at the Dead House. Maybe it was a good thing Chloe was gone. I thought maybe I should text her and suggest she stay gone until I got to the bottom of this paranormal mystery. I could sage the house, which might make the atmosphere feel a little better.

As a young medium, Chloe was working on her skills

for helping the dead move on. I didn't have her kind of skills, but I knew how to investigate, and I could use a ghost box as good as anyone. I sighed as I rolled over on my side. An odd movement caught my eye.

Strange dark shadows gathered in the corner of my room. Remaining very still, I stared at it and as always began debunking what I was experiencing. As the shadows gathered, I could come up with no reason for seeing this particular paranormal manifestation.

Please don't be shadow people. Please don't be shadow people.

I wasn't afraid of much in the way of ghosts, but shadow people were something else entirely, more along the lines of the demonic, not dead people. The shadows in my room collected themselves and became a shape quickly. What I was seeing was oddly formed, like a small whirlwind or a dust devil.

I didn't move and held my breath, hoping that whatever this was wouldn't realize I was awake, which was pretty stupid. That never worked.

Ghosts always knew when you saw them. One did not accidentally stumble upon a ghost. If you saw them, they wanted you to, and if they wanted you to see them, it was because they wanted to connect with you. Usually, they needed your help. A few mean ones just wanted to scare the hell out of you.

I continued to pretend to sleep, and I watched through partially closed eyes as the shadows shifted yet again. The twisting shadow devil crawled up the gray painted wall and spread out across the ceiling as it rose.

It's now or never, Tamara! You've gotta move, girl!

As the shadows touched the ceiling, I opened my eyes to get a better view. It was easier to see it on the white ceiling. The manifestation was not a swirling, dust devil anymore. It folded in on itself and took the shape of a person, a dead person...maybe.

It didn't appear to be an inhuman entity. It had two legs and two arms, a head, and long, stringy black hair. Very long hair that hung down vertically from the ceiling.

As I watched, the hair grew longer and longer. My voice didn't want to work. All I could do was continue to stare in horror as the stringy hair reached for me like living tendrils of blackness. When I could finally move, I sat up and stared into the eyes of the ghost.

There was no sense in pretending we didn't see one another.

I still couldn't speak. I couldn't do much at all but stare above me as the features in the shadow's face began to form. Out of nowhere, Tina Louise's voice popped into my head. This was twice in one day!

What the hell are you doing? Run, idiot!

I rolled out of bed and landed inelegantly on the floor with a loud thud. I wasted not a second climbing to my feet and racing for the door. I ran to the living room and turned on every light I could along the way.

"Joey! Get in here! Where are you?" I heard a light tapping sound on the other side of the front door, but it stopped as quickly as it began. It must have been the wind tossing leaves up on the porch. Joey had been telling me the truth, and I had offered him no comfort. He was right. I was the worst best friend ever.

I guess his cold shoulder was his way of returning the favor. I couldn't deny it any longer.

The Dead House had a new resident.

3

CHLOE

Mom's birthday came and went, and Tamara didn't mention anything about it. If she did remember mom's special day, she didn't let on. At first, I thought maybe she wasn't saying anything because she didn't want to make me sad. You know, stir up grief or something. But I gave her plenty of clues to the contrary. Like always, Tamara wasn't great at picking up my subtle cues.

I baked cupcakes for the occasion complete with sprinkles, and still I heard not a word from her about Mom. She gobbled up the snacks without even asking why I'd spent the day baking and frosting. It occurred to me after she scarfed them down that she didn't remember. This wasn't about avoiding hurting my feelings. This was about her forgetting Mom's birthday.

You would think Mom's best friend would remember. Tamara was always going on about how my mother had been her closest pal and whatnot, but she couldn't even be bothered to celebrate her birthday. Wasn't it on her calendar?

That hurt. It gave me another reason to not like her. That's all I needed, one more reason. Tamara had been nothing but nice to me from the get-go, so situation normal.

Tamara tried really hard, and I didn't try at all.

Maybe my best friend Lynn was right and I should see a therapist. Obviously, I could not hide my feelings forever. At least I had Lynn to talk to. We had only known each other for a few months, but we'd gotten pretty close in that short amount of time. I had friends before, at my old school, but not anyone as close as Lynn and me. I'd always been kind of a loner.

We liked the same music and read the same books. We were the same in a lot of ways but also very different, as I was beginning to discover.

I didn't mind that she recently began hanging out with the "Goth Girls" at school, her former enemies, but that didn't mean I had to like them too. On the other hand, who was I to tell her who she could hang out with? I wasn't that kind of friend, the kind who demanded all your time or forced you to ditch everyone else. I wasn't that insecure.

Lynn had developed some disturbing new habits, though, like posting crazy stuff on that stupid blog of hers and poetry that went a bit too dark for my taste. I understood the poetry, like her obsession with drawing on her skin with permanent markers, were just cries for attention. She was asking for help, and there were times I considered telling someone, but who?

Tamara or Mrs. Brooklyn, the school guidance counselor? I wondered if I could do it anonymously. I wasn't sure how that kind of report worked, but I'd have to do something. What if I lost her friendship? I only had two friends, Lynn and Trey, and I guess that was by choice.

Joey wanted to be on the list, but he was too unpredictable to be a friend. I knew for a fact Joey spied on me when I hung out with Trey. There was nothing worse than making out with your almost-boyfriend and seeing the Ghost in the doorway of the closet with his hand on his hip and a doo-rag on his head.

I even caught him fumbling around in my makeup drawer recently. I couldn't have that, so I reestablished my boundaries by burning sage and meditating in my room.

I was better at it now. In the beginning, I had a difficult time with the visualization aspect. I sent light in all directions, and scattered energy rather than collected it. It wasn't my fault I was an untrained medium. The only way I would get better was to practice. From what I had read, meditation was the best way to protect myself. However, my meditation and "woo-woo" stuff as he called it, didn't harm him anymore. I focused my energy work on my own body and the barrier around my room.

Too bad it didn't work against living jerks like Trey. I kind of missed him, even though I would never admit that to a living soul.

Once upon a time, I believed Trey and I would become a little more than friends, but now I wasn't so sure. We rarely kissed anymore, and we never did anything cool together like hanging out and watch movies or go to the mall.

His latest obsession had taken over his life. Trey had a new hobby—sprucing up an old clunker his dad gave him. The plan was to flip the vehicle for a good chunk of change and then they would split the profit, but that required considerable improvements. The only thing was, Trey's father never helped with any of those so-called improvements. He left it all up to his son, and Trey acted as if he didn't mind at all. I'd only met his father a few times, but we had never engaged in conversation. I got weird vibes from him, and I was polite even though it ticked me off Trey was getting the short end of the stick.

Unfortunately for Trey, I had absolutely no interest in helping him fix up the classic car; the dang thing came with an odd presence. I didn't even want to sit in it, but being the supportive friend I was, I did.

But only once.

In my opinion, the car was a hunk of junk, with possibly major negative energy attached to it. Trey had a perfectly good car already, but my sometimes boyfriend's obsession with the classic Chevy Nova was unbelievably strong. It bordered on becoming a problem.

Then again, who was I to say? I didn't have one car, much less two of them.

Life revolved quickly around me, but I didn't feel as if I were a part of the movement. I was stuck in my own emotional mud. I still missed Mom so much it made me sick sometimes. I wanted to feel better, but it was an exercise in futility.

Every night before bed, I flipped through my Mom's postcards, the ones I had discovered in the attic. I studied her faint script and memorized the exotic locations pictured on those worn cards. I raided Mom's trunk a few more times since that first occasion and found other interesting items I kept as my own treasures. Despite my best efforts, I was no closer to making real contact with her.

Some medium. I couldn't even make a connection with my own mother.

It was as if she had nothing to say to me; like she rejected me again, even in death. I should be used to that by now.

"Chloe? Are you listening to me? We both have to focus on the crystal. That's how this works. It will work if we both focus. Together we have the power to make contact with Tina Louise!"

Lynn recently used a blue rinse on her hair, but the color didn't look great on her. I was too much of a friend to tell her. If I had to guess, I would say her experimenting with the odd color is what had her grounded for a few weeks.

Poor Lynn.

She went from one grounding to the next, and she didn't really do much at all. She was seeking her individuality, just like the rest of us teenagers. At heart, I didn't believe Lynn was a troublemaker. I got the feeling her mother didn't care what she did and in fact, Lynn's mom wasn't around at the moment. Lynn's dad was frequently out of town on his truck driving gig, so my friend was enjoying a few nights of freedom and a break from staying home all the time. At least for a little while.

Earlier, Lynn and I walked over to the Burger Shack and returned with a sack of bad food. After gorging on French fries and soggy hamburgers, my best friend suggested we try a pendulum session. Apparently, it was kind of like a séance, but instead of hovering around a crystal ball or staring at a candle, the participants focus their attention on a crystal pendant.

Things were boring as hell at my house. It wasn't much more exciting here, but at least I got to hang out with Lynn. I just wished she was more like she'd been when we first met, happy go lucky, and outgoing. We couldn't both be depressed.

Here we were, two Debbie-downers hanging out in a stuffy bedroom doing preteen crap.

I could feel Lynn's extreme emotions at times. Whether it was an extrasensory gift from being a medium or just the intuition of a friend I couldn't say, but I sensed she was very lonely, and she was experiencing some strange sort of desperation.

I shook off those awkward feelings and reminded myself not to snoop and to remain in the moment.

"I am focusing, but I'm not sure I like this, Lynn. This feels kind of off. Forbidden. Mediums have to be careful about which methods they use when communicating. I am too open for this, I think."

"Big baby. You have to try it at least once to know for sure." Lynn coerced me to try again. She rebelled against everything and everyone. At least I was kind of quiet about my rebellion. I liked it that way.

"What exactly am I supposed to be focusing on? The crystal? Your voice? The paper?" This wasn't how I wanted to spend my Friday night. The feeling of wrongness increased but I didn't want to disappoint my friend.

Lynn waved the crystal pendant over a piece of paper on which she'd written YES and NO.

"See? You just hold the pendulum still, and it will swing

when you ask it questions. It will probably work better for you since you are an actual medium. Want to give it a try?"

"I don't know, Lynn. It sounds kind of sketchy to me. Wouldn't my unconscious mind move the pendulum? Like I said, I have a bad feeling about this." I did not make any move to accept the hanging crystal from her fingers. I wanted nothing more than to get out of this room.

"Is it cold in here or is it just me?"

Lynn tilted her head and studied me with a frown. "Nice try. Now take the pendulum and ask a question. You heard me. I've tried to engage her with a variety of questions but apparently your mother doesn't want to talk with me. She will probably talk to you, though, if you give her a chance. Isn't that why we're doing this, Chloe? Don't you want to talk to her?" She continued to hold out the end of the string to me, but I was leery about accepting it. I wanted to make a connection with my mother but not like this. I had hoped to use my own abilities, not some home-made Ouija board.

Even thinking about touching the crystal made me sick. To make matters worse, I saw an odd vibration surrounding Lynn. A black aura grew around my friend's head like a deathly halo. Death? What was going on here?

Before I could ask her to stop or warn her about what I saw, the front door slammed downstairs.

"Lynn! Where are you?"

"Shit! It's my dad!" Lynn whispered as she dropped the crystal into my shaking hand. "He's not supposed to be home yet. Damn! And I'm wearing all this makeup. He's going to freak out on me! He's going to totally freak. Be quiet, Chloe. You have to be really quiet. I don't want him to know you're here. I'm not supposed to have friends over while he's gone." As my friend climbed to her feet, she blew out the candle and raced to her bedroom door. "Don't move, or he will hear the floor squeak."

"Got it," I whispered as I reached for my backpack and dug in my back pocket for my cell phone. It wasn't there! My fight or flight impulse was kicking in, but flight was definitely stronger. What was I going to fight?

The black aura around Lynn grew, and it was beginning to fill the room. Her father was stomping up the stairs, and the sound of his voice wasn't friendly at all.

Where was my phone?

"Damn! He's coming to my room. Out the window, Chloe. You have to go out the window and take the trellis down! I'm sorry, but you have to go. I won't be able to protect you if he finds you here. He's drunk, I can tell. I can hear it in his voice." Lynn's hand was on the door.

I whimpered as I considered her proposal.

Me, climb down the side of the house?

There was no time to argue with Lynn and the way her father was roaring, he wasn't the kind of guy to be reasoned with.

"Where are you, girl? Your ass better be in this house! You better be..." Jack let out a string of shocking profanities, and a loud boom indicated that he fell. Unfortunately, it did not injure him, not seriously, because he roared her name again.

In a whisper, I pleaded with her, "How am I supposed to get home? I can't find my phone!"

"Get out of here, Chloe! I'll try to keep him away as long as possible." She slipped out of the bedroom and closed the door behind her. "I'm here, Dad." He continued to swear at her, and I heard her use similar language. I'd heard her swear before, but this was pretty extreme. I could feel the horrible hatred between the two of them...and something else.

Suddenly, I felt I had to go, with or without my cell phone. If I could get out without falling off the side of the house, I would find my way to a safe place. I had some change in my backpack. What were the chances I could find an old-fashioned payphone on this block? If I could remember my house phone. I didn't remember seeing a payphone. I couldn't remember if I'd ever seen one in real life.

I could go to Trey's house.

I smothered a moan while I struggled to get the window up. The dang thing finally broke free, but it made a lot of noise. Luckily for me, but unluckily for Lynn, she and her dad were screaming at one another.

How could I leave my best friend to face that crazy man alone?

I paused before throwing my leg over the sill. Lynn screamed in pain, and more of her father's swearing followed the sound of another crash. Lynn's father was beating the hell out of her. I wasn't going to leave her to die at the hands of a madman. Before I could pivot myself back into the room, I felt hands shoving me back out.

It freaked me out so badly I didn't even consider going back inside. I know I felt hands on me!

A voice threatened me. The thing that lived here with Lynn and her father Jack knew who I was, and it didn't like me being here. This was the black aura, the negative energy source that had grown so strong it had its own voice.

Get out!

I swore as I clambered down the shrubby green vines that covered the side of Lynn's family home. I heard her swearing back at him, so she must be okay. No matter what, I was calling the cops as soon as I got down.

Don't look down. Don't look down, Chloe!

I forgot how much I hated heights. I couldn't even get on a ladder without feeling nauseated, and here I was clambering down the side of a house in the middle of the night.

No time to reflect on my bad choices. I needed to focus on getting down. The vine didn't feel too steady, and neither did the wooden lattice it clung to. I wasn't sure I was going to make it. Ten feet left. I couldn't look down again. Bad idea, bad idea. I slung the backpack up on my shoulder and continued my journey down.

It was pitch-black outside, and there was no light on the side of Lynn's house. I had to be close to the bottom, but I couldn't make myself look. I just couldn't do it. I bit my lip as I closed my eyes and felt around for the next handhold.

That was when I felt the hands on me again. I nearly screamed but remembered to keep quiet. I cocked my head around and breathed a sigh of relief as Trey's face came into view.

"It's me. Let's get out of here, Chloe. Uncle Jack is dangerous when he's drunk. Follow me." Trey took my hand and led me out of the yard. We scurried away, bent over to keep our head beneath the hedgerow. I scurried into the garage and hugged Trey as I caught my breath. He held me tight, and I took comfort in his arms. "You okay? Did he hurt you?"

I glanced up at him. "No, but Lynn, Trey. I'm sure he's hurting Lynn. Someone needs to know! We have to call the cops," I begged as the garage darkened and the heavy door closed slowly behind me.

"No cops, Chloe. We've tried that before. They won't do a damn thing, and it will only be worse for her afterward." He released me and shook his head sadly. I stared at him in disbelief and watched as his silhouette darkened.

"You don't understand. I seriously think he's going to kill her, Trey."

He swore under his breath and said, "You stay here, Chloe. I'll try to calm him down. No matter what you hear, stay here—and no cops."

"I can't let you go over there by yourself. Your uncle sounds really drunk. He's on a rampage! You have to call someone!"

Trey took my hand. "You don't understand who I am, who we are, Chloe. You don't understand my family. We have a reputation in Crystal Springs. Too notorious to call the cops. Just stay here. I'll take you home after I deal with this. Follow me."

Trey led me into his house, and I was shocked again at the bareness of the place. I'd been here before, but we usually hung around in the kitchen or the garage. My home, the Ridaught Plantation, had more than enough furniture, dusty old couches, oversized dressers. This place had nothing much at all except a few bar stools, a bare wooden spool that once held some kind of cable and there was a television in the corner of the room, and a lumpy couch. Talk about depressing.

"Okay, but be careful," I whispered as I clutched my backpack tightly. "I warn you, if you're not back in five minutes, I'm calling the police."

"Five minutes," he echoed as he went out the front door. "I'll be back, but stay here."

I agreed and stood awkwardly in the kitchen as I waited for the other shoe to drop. Maybe I should go ahead and call Tamara now and fill her in on what was happening. A quick visual sweep of the kitchen revealed there was no telephone, no way to call out. Was there even a phone in this house? I'd left mine behind in Lynn's bedroom, or somewhere. I couldn't be sure.

I knew it was bad manners to go poking around Trey's place when he specifically asked me to remain in the kitchen, but I needed to find a phone. I was serious about calling someone if he wasn't back in five minutes. At the very least, I would call Tamara.

True to his word Trey returned rather quickly, but he didn't stick around long. He looked like he'd been fighting, his face was red, and his hair mussed. Lynn came in and collapsed beside me on the couch.

"Here, I found your phone."

I took it from her, but she fell into my arms and cried her heart out. Luckily, I heard her father's big truck crank up next door. Trey went outside and had words with him. I couldn't hear what they were, but they weren't polite.

"Did he hurt you?"

"Nothing hurts anymore," she confessed as she lay on the couch beside me.

"Should I leave? I can call Tamara. We can both go to my place."

Lynn dabbed her eyes with her ink-stained fingers. "No. That'll just make it worse for me. I have to stay, but you can go. I'll understand."

I shook my head. "Nope. Not leaving you. Let's just hunker down here on the couch. It doesn't sound like Trey's coming in. He's working on that car again."

"Thanks, Chloe Carol. You are a good friend. A true-blue friend."

"You're welcome. And so are you."

We talked a little while, not about her jerk of a father but about the future. About leaving Crystal Springs and starting a new life somewhere else, maybe as an artist. That was her dream. I didn't really have a dream. Maybe one day.

Soon Lynn was snoring, and I spent the night jumping at every sound. Trey came inside about two in the morning, but he didn't pay me a bit of attention.

He wasn't alone.

The black aura that had attached itself to Lynn earlier was dogging his steps now. He went to his room and closed the door. I breathed a sigh of relief, and right before dawn, I fell asleep.

4

TAMARA

I'd gotten up early and added quite a bit more material to the outline despite the fact I tossed and turned all night after the visitation. Before I headed to the office, I tried to grab some EVPs and check the electromagnetic field, but there was nothing unusual to report. It was as if I'd imagined it, but there was no damn way.

After my failed grab for clues to help classify the activity, I shifted gears. I sucked down a few cups of coffee and tentatively plotted out my book. Originally, I had thought Monday would be a good day to dive in; now I wasn't so sure. After an hour of typing and deleting notes on my laptop, I got up to work on other things.

I had a small painting project to tackle, and I needed to make a grocery list.

I took the table outside and scraped the old paint off and neatly recovered it with clean, blue paint. The table was a yard sale find, and I was excited about freshening it up. I didn't pay much for it, but by the time I was done, I would have quite a bit of sweat equity tied up in it, and it felt good to work with my hands.

Between paint applications, I decided to open all the windows on the lower level. It was time to let in some fresh air. As I headed back out, I caught the chandelier moving again, slowly spinning to the left and to the right. The crystals tinkled under the power of an invisible wind. There was no significant breeze today, so what could make this thing move like that?

I glanced around. The mail on the foyer table wasn't moving. My half-dead plant beside the mail stack wasn't budging either. Then the chandelier stopped again.

I'd have to go upstairs eventually and check out the connector. The last thing I needed was to have a chandelier come crashing down on us. I pushed the troubling thought aside and breathed a sigh of relief, knowing I would check a few things off my own to-do list today.

That was the single life for you. The only honey-dos I had were the honey-do-it-yourself kind.

I was feeling pretty good about my progress until the neighbor's cat descended on my freshly painted table. I'd left the table in the yard to grab a glass of tea when I spotted the animal from the window. For a brief second, I believed the feline perpetrator was a ghost, it looked so much like the cat Joey toted around occasionally.

Nope. It was Miss Linda's pet and it had totally messed up my paint job. The furry rascal would have blue paws for a while. No doubt she'll stomp over here and complain, but it served him right.

After chasing the animal away, I tried to touch up the tabletop, but it was useless. The paw prints were permanent. That rascal had picked the perfect time to destroy my work. I'd have to start over but not right now.

It was time to move on to my next project, making that call to the publishing company. I wondered if they were open on weekends. After cleaning my brushes and putting my paint away, I decided to first tackle planting flowers in the clay pots on my porch. I was really stalling. Did I think the letter was a prank?

Later I would spend time with Chloe. I thought she'd be home by now, but ten o'clock rolled around and Chloe wasn't home yet.

I'd gotten up early this morning, a new habit I was trying to embrace. I never thought I would be a morning person, but here at Crystal Springs, I was turning over a new leaf, trying to be an adult and whatnot.

I walked back inside and washed the dirt off my hands. I sipped the rest of my tea and talked to myself. Actually, I was talking to Joey, hoping he'd show up, but he was nowhere to be seen.

No Chloe. No Joey.

I thought maybe I should just get out of the house a while. I really needed to make a grocery store trip, and I'd been planning on visiting the unexplored section at the back of the property. Maybe I would do that and then do the grocery shopping.

I put my glass in the sink and paused as I listened to a familiar noise upstairs. I didn't know how Chloe got here without me knowing it. Undoubtedly, she was home because I could hear the upstairs shower running. I paused to listen more intently. That was definitely the shower. The pipes rattled.

Had Lynn pulled into the driveway without me seeing or hearing her? I guessed it was possible even though Lynn's car was louder than mine.

I really needed to buy Chloe a vehicle so she could come and go without relying on her friends for a ride, and since I had potentially landed a publishing deal, it might be possible without tapping into her trust fund. After some hemming and hawing, I called Bright House and left a polite voicemail, but as I suspected, they were closed on the weekends.

Chloe might have a chip on her shoulder about life—and me—but overall, Chloe Carol was a good teenager. She was a good kid. Tina Louise would be proud of her.

I might as well bring her laundry up since I was about to put my last load in. I grabbed a stack of Chloe's lavender towels and her neatly folded shirts. "Chloe!" I called her name as I went upstairs to annoy her through the bathroom door. As soon as I began climbing the stairs, the hair on my arms began to rise as if I'd rubbed one of those old-fashioned static balls, like the kind I used to toy with at the Monroeville Museum. Static electricity was all over my body, and it was a weird sensation.

"Chloe?" I said in an attempt to feel normal, and feel safe despite the increased electrical discharge. It wasn't like these stairs were carpeted, and I wasn't wearing shoes, just thin socks. I had every intention to sweep the floors at some point this weekend, also on my general to-do list. My ever-growing to-do list.

As I climbed the stairs, the lights flickered, and I paused on the staircase. The lights flickered two more times and then all was normal again.

The upstairs shower was definitely running. It had to be Chloe unless it was Joey pulling a prank to get a rise out of me. He was definitely not happy with me.

I hurried up the staircase and waited outside the door for a minute. I wasn't sure Chloe could even hear me with the shower running. It sounded as if it was on full blast and I could see steam coming out from under the door. Why was my body tingling? I tapped on the door and waited for her response.

"Chloe? It's me. I have fresh towels. Do you need one?"

I expected her to mumble a complaint or tell me to get lost, but neither one of those things happened. Steam rolled out from under the door like an ominous fog.

"Chloe? Are you okay in there?" I knocked on the door again, pretending I wasn't feeling tremendously creeped out.

I heard the shower stop. I even heard the knobs squeaking like Chloe had turned them off. Maybe she didn't answer because she hadn't heard me.

"Hey, it's me. Can I come in? Should I just leave the towels out here?" I heard nothing except the faintest whisper behind me. Twisting my neck ever so slightly, I peeked to my left in the direction of the voice, but the hallway was empty.

"Joey, you better not be screwing with me. Cut it out."

Joey did not appear, and I heard no further whispers. I waited to hear the shower curtain slide open. It didn't happen. Not a dang sound. Nothing at all. After a few seconds, I couldn't stand it anymore. I had to make sure Chloe was okay. The door squeaked as I inched it open politely.

"Chloe? It's me." I clutched the warm towels to my chest and whispered her name again. I flipped the light on immediately even though the room was bright and cheerful. There was a high window above the shower. The bathroom had so much steam in it I could barely see. The curtain remained pulled wide so I couldn't see anyone in the shower. The steam swirled above the curtain, and I watched it creep up and out of the room. There wasn't a sound. I set the towels on the vanity and swatted at the steam.

"Chloe? It's me. I brought towels."

I wasn't talking to anyone. Chloe wasn't in here. That curtain was still pulled. Did I really want to sling that puppy back? I didn't know why Chloe would be hanging out in the shower, ignoring me. The faucet dripped, and the steamy air swirled around me.

"Joey? This better not be one of your stupid pranks. Step out of that shower now!" I threatened my ghostly best friend in the most serious tone I could muster, but he didn't poke his head out. There wasn't a sound to be heard except the dripping of water. I took a step toward the shower as the steam quickly dissipated through the open door. Why wasn't this a glass shower door?

I thought I saw the curtain move, a slight fluttering of fabric. Chloe's sugar skull shower curtain wasn't putting my heart and mind at ease, but this was her bathroom, so I hadn't made a fuss when she came home with it the other day.

"Joey? Is that you? Don't be a jerk."

I was only a few inches from the shower curtain now. How many horror movies had I watched that started like this? But I was a paranormal investigator. It's my job to look, to debunk, to search out the answer. I had to see for myself who was in here.

My fingers shook as I cautiously reached for the fabric. Holding my breath, I slung the curtain back.

There was no one there. The shower was empty, but the faucet dripped and the steam rolled around me as if to testify to the truth. I wasn't alone here. I quickly screwed the faucets off completely. The spirit had left the water dripping. I drew back and away from the shower. As my brain attempted to ponder the possibilities, the bathroom door behind me slammed shut with a vengeance.

A string of expletives flew out of my mouth as I clutched my heart and I immediately opened the door. I was pissed off now. Running into the hallway, I spun around looking for who had been in that shower.

"Joey? Are you here?"

The doorbell rang, and as there was no response, I jetted to the front door, hoping my unexpected visitor wasn't my neighbor. Or a drenched spirit with very long black hair. It sure wouldn't be Chloe unless she lost her key, which wouldn't be the first time. With one quick glance over my shoulder, I opened the door.

I was surprised to find Kevin on my porch.

"Kevin? What are you doing here? Did Linda call you again?"

Talk about a déjà vu moment.

The deputy smiled politely and cleared his throat. "No. May I come inside? Before Linda does show up? I'd like to talk to you privately if you have a few minutes." Since he had a folder in his hand, I assumed whatever was in it was what he wanted to talk about. Call me curious. Who was I to close the door on a mystery? Or Deputy Kevin Patrick.

"Sure," I said as I opened the door and welcomed him inside. He thoughtfully wiped his shoes on my doormat, and I invited him to join me in the kitchen. He'd been here before, but his last visit had been a while. "Want something to drink? Coffee maybe? I've got tea if you prefer that."

"No, thanks. I'm good." Kevin sat at the kitchen table and put the folder in front of him. I took the seat across from him. It had been a while since we chatted, and I suddenly realized I was happy to see him. Probably too happy.

"What do you have there? Another cold case?" It was a guess but apparently a good one. Kevin's sulky bedroom eyes met mine, but his voice was deep and serious. He casually opened the folder and spun it around to show me the photo on top.

"Yes, it's another cold case, and I'm hoping you'll help me with it. Meet Aaron Knight." He slid the photo out of the folder and pushed it across the table. A sad feeling came over me as I stared at the young face that looked back at me from the faded black and white photo. I carefully touched the edge of the picture with my fingers. It made me feel sorrowful. That was the word.

I had so many questions, and I wasn't sure which one to ask first.

"He's so young," I whispered as I picked up the picture and studied it. "How did he die?"

Kevin studied the form in the folder. "Asphyxiation. He was twenty-five when he died and a student at a community college in the next county. He died in 1997."

That was heartbreaking to hear. I didn't know why Kevin was showing me this. He didn't believe in psychics and such, not really. Did he think I pulled Annie's killer's name out of the air?

"That's tragic. Did he die here? Is that why you're here?" I bit my lip as I stared at the young man's face. He had an angular jawline, and his eyes were dark and a bit large for his narrow face. His tousled hair was carefully styled with too much gel, but then again, that had been the style in the late 90s. Poor Aaron Knight. To die so young.

"Aaron died on the road behind this house. He was found in his car with a scarf around his neck, murdered and left for dead. I need to find his killer. My boss, Sheriff Jarvis, he's counting on me to find the truth. I'd like you to help me."

I slid the picture back to Kevin and swallowed the lump in my throat. I knew this face. I'd seen it in my dream. More than once too. "You're welcome to search the premises if you think you'll find anything. I'll help however I can and I'm sure Chloe wouldn't mind either."

He put his hat on the table. "I'd like your help. Your unique help."

"My unique help? What exactly are you asking me?"

To my surprise, Deputy Kevin reached across the table and briefly tapped my hand. It wasn't quite a squeeze and not anything that would technically be described as flirtatious, but it surprised me.

"I know all about you, Tamara Garvey."

"You do?" I asked breathlessly.

"Probably more than you want me to know. I'm here to ask you to use your skills as a paranormal investigator to help me find Aaron's killer. You were a paranormal investigator, correct?"

"Yes. That's correct." I couldn't help but wonder what he meant by saying he knew all about me. Was he saying he knew I used to be a burlesque dancer? If he thought I was going to be ashamed or embarrassed, he had another think coming. He closed the folder and leaned back in the chair, studying me as if I were a suspect and this was an interrogation.

Just hear him out, and don't be so judgmental, I told myself. Maybe he was telling the truth and he just wants your help. I decided to take my own advice for once.

"What exactly did you have in mind?"

"I want you to try to make contact with Aaron. Of course, I can't ask you to do that on an official level because...well...you know why. But as a friend, I'm asking you to do this for Aaron. For this young man."

"Of course, I'll help Aaron. Of course, I want to know who killed him. That's the kind of person I am. But I am not a psychic. I am an investigator, and there is a huge difference between the two. Sometimes I get lucky and I can talk to the dead through my equipment. Tell you what, I'll try to reach out to this guy, and if I hear anything, I'll let you know. But it's my turn to ask you a question."

The handsome deputy leaned forward and propped his chin on his folded hands. "Ask away. I'm an open book, Tamara."

"Why? Why is this case so important to your sheriff? The guy's been dead for over fifteen years. I'm just curious as to why."

"Because Sheriff Jarvis is dying. The treatments aren't

helping at all. He asked me to do this for him, and he doesn't have long. These cases mean a lot to him, and he doesn't want to leave this world knowing he has no answers for the families. That's why in a nutshell." The deputy rose from his table. "I'll leave you this folder. That's your copy."

"Oh, sorry. I hate to hear that about anyone. I'm really...I'll do what I can, Kevin."

"I know you will. You're a good person. I believe that. God knows we've exhausted all our leads. I've been through that folder backward and forward. I don't want to give too much away, but let's just say Aaron was no choir boy. Still, he deserves justice."

I wondered if I should tell him I was working on another book, and this felt similar to the story I was writing, and to my dreams. I might as well come clean. I'd rather do it now than later. All I needed was for a murder case to come back and bite me in the ass.

"I feel like I need to tell you this. I've been writing about Aaron already. Yes, it's true. I didn't know his name, but I think this is the guy I've been dreaming about. He was choking and had such bad pain in his neck. I don't think he was alone. He was looking for someone. That's what I felt in the dream. I just wanted you to know."

Kevin shook his head and rubbed his temples before letting out a deep sigh. "I can't stop you from writing about Aaron, but I would ask you to protect his name and identity. If you are tuning into that other world, it has to be a good thing. Maybe Aaron knows we're trying to figure it out, and he's trying to help us." He smiled as we walked to the door. "Now I sound like a crazy person. I'm not sure

Sheriff Jarvis would approve of me bringing you in on the conversation, but it is what it is. Keep me posted, please. I'll continue to work the leads I have, which are, sadly, very few. Thanks, Tamara." The deputy stepped out on the porch, and I walked out with him.

"You're welcome. I hope I can help. When this is over, you owe me a beer."

He paused at his vehicle and opened the door. He smiled sadly at me. "When this is over, I'll probably owe you more than that. Later."

With a weird mixture of sadness and excitement, I watched him drive away.

5

MRS. LOPER

The rain continued to fall as it had for days. I lost track of how many. The monotony of life saddened me. That was not accurate. Sad was not strong enough of a word to describe my emotions as I continued to study the rain. Sheets of water slid down the windows whereas before fat droplets pelted the glass.

How much rain could the heavens hold? Was that all one could expect to find in heaven, endless buckets of water? No matter, I would never walk through those pearly gates. I would spend my eternal existence somewhere else. I was sure of it. That did not frighten me. I felt no fear anymore.

Only this gray sadness.

From my vantage point on the second floor of the plantation, I could see a great deal of the property, but the rain obscured the view. I could not observe the road at all.

Mr. Loper would return soon or so he had promised before he left yesterday. Every time he left, I always felt as if he would never return.

Maybe for our daughters, he would return. He loved Betsy and Annabel with all his might. He would come back with medicines, a cure of some sort, or maybe even the doctor. It had been silly to leave. It was only a fever. Children recovered from fevers all the time and we had strong girls.

Strong like me.

Strong like my sister too. And our mother. I chewed my fingernail as I continued to stare into the wall of water. One of the girls was crying, but I did not comfort her. I was never very good at comforting. That had been my sister's talent. She comforted, and I did other things. Like squeezed birds until they died. I did not trust myself to handle my children, for Mr. Loper loved them very much, and above all else, I wanted and desired my husband's love.

I had killed for it, hadn't I? No, I would not handle the children.

That was Anita's job, not mine. Besides, what if they made me sick too? I could not risk such a thing for that would further separate me from Mr. Loper. I pondered it daily. How would I do it? To take one's life with poison was easy. If I were to die by my own hand, I would do so much more dramatically. My sin demanded it.

Maybe I should die while he was gone. His harsh words rang in my ears. It had suddenly blown up between us. He made his raw confession and I could barely believe what he said.

"I know what you've done, Alice. Or should I call you Lavinia? I have always known, since almost the beginning, but for your sister's sake, I kept you as my wife. Now shut up and do not speak of it again."

Andrew had stabbed the table with a dinner fork, and I said nothing else. He continued to call me Mrs. Loper, as everyone knew me, and even in private, he called me Mrs. Loper. No more Alice.

Betsy cried and called for me, but I did not go to the nursery.

Most fevers were harmless, but I had heard that occasionally, sudden fevers snuffed out entire families. Sickness could strike an entire community, even those that did not live close together. The invisible could kill, and the invisible had no mercy.

Our large and lovely mansion was quite separated from the smaller homes surrounding it, but there was always the risk of contamination. Which was why I insisted Anita stay with me and not leave. If she were to return home to her family and her little shack in the slave's quarters, she would surely return with the plague.

As I chewed my fingernail down to the quick, I imagined in my mind how I should die again. No, I wanted to live to see Andrew, didn't I? I glanced over my shoulder and stared into the dingy mirror beside me. I saw not my own face but my sister, the true Alice. My own twin, dead, by my hand. Dead so I could steal her destiny. Had it been five years? Six?

I should pay for my crimes!

My hands began to shake as I recalled those heinous memories. I turned away from the rain-drenched landscape and covered my mouth with my hand for fear I would scream to the heavens and confess my heavy soul to whoever may hear it. Perhaps then I could beg for mercy, but to do so, to speak those things out loud would admit the thing I wanted most to keep secret. And I must do that. Even if it cost me my soul.

Andrew knew. He had known a long time. He was lost to me. He no longer called me by my sister's name. I was no longer his sweet Alice.

We all have our secrets, don't we, sister?

Go away, Alice. You are not alive. I am Alice now!

I kept my eyes closed, but I waved at the space beside me as if the dead woman were truly there.

As quietly as any mouse, Anita had stepped into the room. She was a thin, nervous woman with skin as dark as any I had ever seen. She had a feminine voice and a kind way about her that made me want to trust her even though I found it very difficult to do.

Trusting people was a weakness, and one I could not afford even as my heart yearned for understanding.

"Mrs. Loper, are you feeling all right, ma'am? Why don't you come eat a bite or two? Just a bite of something to keep your strength up. Please, Mrs. Loper. If you get sick, it will do no one any good. Those babies need you. Don't you worry. Mr. Loper will return soon."

Anita always brought me comfort. Ever since my arrival here, she had taken me under her wing as if I were her own daughter. What a foolish thing to believe a slave would think of me as a daughter, but what did I know of mothers and daughters? Although I didn't deserve such affection, I did not reject it either. It did not seem strange to me that she was black, and I was white or that I felt she loved me. It did not seem strange to me that she knew more about my husband than I did.

I was a lost little angel, she told me quite often in the

beginning, but the truth was quite different, and I think she knew that now. More like a lost little devil. Despite her error, I appreciated her cautious love and concern.

"No, thank you. I must keep watch for Mr. Loper. He could return anytime. He should've already returned, Anita. I can't understand why he's been gone so long. Our daughters are very sick — they will make us all sick. I thought it was just a fever, but it is the plague, isn't it? It is the plague! What shall we do?" My hands continued to shake, but then the sensation was no longer restricted to my hands and fingers. My entire body began to shake. My teeth began to chatter, and I was freezing. Freezing as if I had been standing inside the icehouse with the door shut. Only moments ago, I was warm, and now I was freezing.

Had Death touched me and marked me for his own? Was I doomed to follow my youngest child into the grave? Many of the slave children had died this past winter, and I heard whispers that Anita's children were sick too. For that I was sorry, but I could not allow her to leave me here. I needed her to comfort me and to watch my children. I needed someone to take care of us. I always needed that.

I was a lost little angel, she said so herself.

Yes, you always need someone, don't you?

Out of the corner of my eye, I saw her still—my sister Alice—and her voice was in my ears. How was it that she was here? I had left her far away in Boston. Far away from my new life, but here she was. I felt her before and imagined her aroma, but this...she grew strong in her anger.

This was different. Somehow Alice had found a way to manifest in the midst of this plague. Oh, she would like me to die, wouldn't she?

"Are you coming down with the fever?" Anita's cool hand touched my forehead and she immediately drew back. "Oh, my goodness, Mrs. Loper. We must get you to bed now. Come on, ma'am. Let's get you into your bed. Don't you worry about your babies. I will take care of them, and I will take care of all of you. You can trust Anita. You can always trust Anita." Her hand gently rubbed my back and I did indeed feel comforted, knowing I was not alone here in this empty palace with the vengeful ghost of my sister. The grand plantation had seemed like a palace when I first arrived with its many rooms and large windows. Now it was my prison.

I missed the crowded streets of Boston. I missed home even though it had not been a loving place. I had never been lonely there.

I never wanted children. I never wanted to be a mother, but as a wife, I had no choice in the matter. Bearing children was my responsibility. Bearing children was part of being a woman; that's what Mr. Loper told me.

I knew I should love my children, but I did not. Not as other mothers loved theirs. No doubt in my own way, I would come to love Betsy and Annabel. I did like that they appeared to be tiny representations of me. They both looked very much like me. Everyone who saw them commented on the likeness. I suppose in some ways, it was very sad for them as I was not a pretty woman. I came from a line of plain women. That's how everyone described Alice and Lavinia.

My daughters were only three and four years old. Our third child, another daughter, had died not long after her birth a few months ago. The baby only lived a few weeks.

Her death had been harder on Mr. Loper than me. I felt a strange sense of relief. Of course, I was wise enough not to share that truth with anyone. Not even with Anita, although I suspected she knew my true feelings.

I hoped I would never have more children, but such things appeared to be out of my control. Mr. Loper enjoyed his conjugal rights, and I understood the connection between childbirth and intimacy. Although, since his confession to me about knowing my true identity, he no longer shared a bed with me.

That is it then. I have lost his love forever. Perhaps when the girls were older, I would love them more. If they lived that long. Maybe when they could help me sew new dresses and curl my hair, I would love them but they were a long way from that.

I felt woozy as Anita struggled with my stays. She'd tied them too tightly this morning, and her old fingers were having a difficult time working the knots.

Oh, but to be free of these heavy garments! At last the skirt fell to the floor, and I stepped out of it and sat on the bed obediently as Anita continued her work. I was down to my petticoats and still sweating as if I'd run a mile in the middle of the summer afternoon.

"You've got the fever. You'll have to stay in this bed, ma'am. Leave it all to me. I will take care of those girls. Betsy and Annabel will be just fine."

They were not fine at all, I thought to myself.

Too often, they whispered to one another. I imagine they plotted against me. Just as Alice and I plotted against our mother. Wretched cow of a woman! At least the girls had a father who loved them and stayed with their mother despite her flaws. Mr. Loper certainly loved them more than he had ever loved me, and he showered them with affection. He brought them gifts and rained kisses down upon them daily.

But they whispered all the time. I did not like that. Betsy and Annabel and all their whispering and giggling. Were they laughing at me? I began to suspect the horrible truth. Our daughters knew about me, they knew my secret.

They knew their mother was not who she said she was, and they would eventually tell the world. It'd been bad luck to have girls. Better to have boys, I thought. I may have loved a boy. Alice and I believed every word to come out of our mother's mouth even though we hated her immensely. Indeed, Alice and I spent much of our time plotting against her.

It had not been my idea to poison the kitten. I did not want to believe that. If I was now Alice, and I was, I could place the blame on Lavinia. Lavinia cut the rope that dropped the bag and crushed Mr. Kennedy. It had been my sister's idea. She was full of bad thoughts and intentions. She whispered them into my ears day and night. Night and day.

Not me. Never me! Mr. Loper would have to believe me. I was Alice Loper! Not Lavinia!

My sister's gray face mocked me from the mirror on the vanity table. Kill them. Kill them while they are small.

"Go away! I am Alice now! You are dead!" I resisted her repeated urgings, but I feared the day would come I could no longer resist her. I feared the day I would not be able to refuse. I feared the day when I shed this Alice skin and became Lavinia again.

When Alice and I first met Mr. Loper, we had a bit of fun with him. It was easy to do since we were twins. Alice would pretend to be me, and I would pretend to be her, and he would court us both. Being twins, it was an easy ruse, one we were quite skilled at, but in the end, I outsmarted my sister and my mother.

And I outsmarted Mr. Loper.

Alice thought for sure Andrew Loper would be hers. That she would marry the very wealthy Mr. Loper and leave me behind with Mother. To my surprise, our mother agreed that indeed Mr. Loper should marry Alice and not me. Why she would choose her side was beyond me as both my sister and I believed our mother hated us equally. Alice thought herself so clever! I wondered what she must've done to garner that endorsement.

Alice and Lavinia Tinsley were not the prettiest girls in Boston, but we were clever. Of the two of us I was the cleverest. I was the clear winner for in the end, I had taken what was mine. It was easy to do.

Because of my past experience, I knew taking a life was far easier than I could have imagined. No! That was Lavinia, not me! I was Alice, always and forever.

Oh, sister, it had been so easy to kill you.

When Alice had no more air, when her eyes bulged and I knew she saw nothing and her last breath released, I slid the ring off her finger and put it on my own. Where it had been every day from that day forward to this one. I rubbed it now to remind myself of my prior victory.

Go away, Alice! You are dead and I am alive!

Anita helped me to bed. I was so cold that even my bones felt cold. The shaking would not stop, and I thought perhaps I would vomit. Vomiting and shaking were both signs of the deathly fever.

Would I die too, along with my daughters?

I gripped Anita's hand desperately and begged her, "Don't let me suffer. I cannot suffer!"

"You ain't gonna die or suffer, Mrs. Loper. You just have a fever is all, girl. You should rest now and let me tend to the little ones. I'll be back soon with a bite for you to eat. You need to keep your strength up and you must drink some water to fight that fever. Stay right here in this bed and don't get up now. You need your rest, child. No more talk."

As she always did whenever someone mentioned death or dying, Anita made strange signs with her fingers, as if to ward off the darkness she feared. Little did she know, I was the darkness she should fear. Darkness lived inside me. I wasn't sure if there was a heaven or if there truly was a hell but no doubt I deserved entrance to the latter.

I must've fallen asleep while waiting for Anita to return. And when I woke, I was covered in sweat. My usually neat bun had collapsed, and much of my wavy hair was stuck to my neck and face. I needed water. Time had certainly passed because it was dark in my room. We were in the middle of the storm, yet I heard no thunder and I saw no lightning, but the rain continued. The relentless, never-ending rain.

Mr. Loper would never return. Perhaps my husband had abandoned me after all. Perhaps he could no longer live with my secret. I had done my best to persuade him he was wrong but there was no talking to him.

"Anita," I whispered in a hoarse voice. "I need water.

Help me, Anita." My eyes were burning, and I could barely see. I tugged at the collar of my flimsy gown and if I had the strength, I would have ripped it from my body. My flesh was so hot I was certain I would burn. I deserved to burn. Burn in eternal hellfire.

I managed to stumble to the small table next to the door of my bedroom. There was a pitcher that usually held water. There was a scant amount in it but no cup. I poured water into my hot hand and put it to my lips. I slurped like a dog and with the remaining drops rubbed my face with the water. Having recovered my voice slightly, I called again, "Anita? Where are you?"

There was no answer. Where was my servant? And Andrew? Would Mr. Loper never return? I was by myself. All alone in this horrible place that had too many rooms and too many memories.

Then I heard a child crying.

Betsy? Annabel? I could not tell. Why would they be crying?

"Anita? The children...why are the children crying?"

There was no answer except for the rain which continued to pound against the windows and the roof. No answer except for the sound of two little girls crying for their mother.

I began to walk down the hall.

6

CHLOE

It felt as if I barely crawled into bed when I felt it shaking. Naturally it was the bane of my existence, the Ghost a.k.a. Joey. "Oh, God. Go away. Why are you in here? I'm pretty sure I revoked your permission to snoop around my room." My barrier must be down.

"There's a ghost in the house, and she's a crazy bitch! Do your thing, Chloe! Get rid of her." I slung the covers back and shielded my eyes with my hand as Joey glowed next to me. Clearly, he was excited about something. He was always a bit luminous, but especially if he was afraid or happy or anything extreme. That's a good word for him. Extreme. Tamara lovingly called him extra from time to time, but I wasn't as generous as she was.

"Pipe down, please." I pulled the covers back over my head, determined to grab forty winks. I hadn't slept much last night. I should've called Tamara right after the hoopla began with Lynn and her father Jack, but I was trying to be a good friend. At least I didn't call the cops. That whole situation was just too weird. Note to self: never spend the night at Lynn's again.

Not to mention Trey and his weirdness. It was like he was a whole other family and that black, pulsating aura...and clowns everywhere. So many pictures of clowns, the old-fashioned kind with the sad eyes and overly painted frowns. Trey told me they belonged to his mother, but like his cousin Lynn, his mother was nowhere around.

"Get out of my room! Seriously. How did you get past my barrier, Joey? Go bother Tamara!"

Joey's voice warbled slightly, giving it a strange under-water sound. "I thought we were friends, Chloe. Tamara ain't here, now be quiet! That crazy ghost is looking for me! She keeps sneaking up on me, calling me Andrew. Scoot over."

I wrapped my blanket around tighter. "Who is Andrew? One of your dates? Don't you dare get in my bed with me! What do you mean, Tamara's not here?" Joey slid under the blanket with me and tried to cuddle. "Cut that out! You're freezing me—don't touch me!" I reached for the lamp, but it didn't come on. The alarm clock wasn't on either. "Is the power out? What's going on? I told you to stop touching me."

"I'm not touching you, cover hog."

Completely awake now, I snatched the covers away from him even harder at the same time I reached my hand into the nightstand drawer beside me. I always kept a flashlight just in case there was a power outage. We had far too many of those lately, and I enjoyed none of them.

Being immersed in darkness in this house always put me on edge. I couldn't say why, but it was as if ghosts preferred the darkness, and as I was a medium, they always came at me when there wasn't light around. Note to self, if I'm ever a ghost, I won't be afraid of light.

It didn't matter a bit, and this was my family home. None of my family had wanted me to know about it. My grandmother sure never spoke about it. Hindsight was 20/20 as they say. I recalled she worked really hard to keep me in the dark when it came to my family's lineage. Until my mother died, I never even knew there was such a place as the Ridaught Plantation. For the life of me I couldn't understand why it was such a big secret. So, what if the locals referred to it as the Dead House? There were certainly dead people here, including one very irritating Joey.

Maybe there was some sort of weird family secret I had not yet uncovered. I loved the Ridaught Plantation more than I expected. Just knowing my mother had been here, that once upon a time, she'd roamed these halls and investigated each room, made me love the family home despite the odd apparition. This was my inheritance.

"Go check it out!"

I guess that meant I inherited Joey too. The truth was he was starting to grow on me, but I wasn't going to tell him that. He'd run over me like he ran over Tamara. Silent lightning popped outside my bedroom window, and it illuminated the room in a strange blue light.

"It's so cold in here."

I clicked on the flashlight and waved it around the room. "That's your fault. Dead people are always cold, and you know it, so quit touching me. Last warning, or I start calling you the Ghost again."

"You promised you wouldn't. Oh, no! She's coming this way. I can feel her. Shut up, loudmouth. She'll hear us in here." Joey's eyes were wide with fear, and like a child, he ducked his head under the covers. Hiding beneath the blanket did little good since he was glowing like that crazy glow worm toy I used to have. I wondered what happened to that thing.

My body experienced an unexpected wave of the chills, and like Joey, I put my head under the covers. I flipped off my flashlight and decided against going to investigate. What was the point?

There was a ghost in the house, and it wasn't Joey.

The floor creaked outside my door. It wasn't unusual for that particular board to creak, but it was unusual for there to be ghosts hanging around in my room. They didn't usually like coming into my sanctum. I worked hard to keep them out. Between saging and crystals and meditation, my room was normally a peaceful oasis compared to other parts of the house, like the attic, and sometimes the back of the property. I still saw lights from time to time, but the Reaper came once in a while and collected them. We never spoke, but I caught sight of him from time to time. At least the Reaper no longer came inside the house.

The creaking stopped, and I heard a woman whispering.

No, not whispering. She was humming a song, a lullaby. A baby cried quietly, but she shushed the child and continued her song. The words were faint at first, but I picked up the tune quickly.

Sleep my child and peace attend thee
All through the night

Guardian angels God will send thee,
All through the night...

"She's going to find me!" Joey whined as he gripped me in his cold embrace like I was some sort of good luck charm. "Don't let her get me, Chloe!"

"Get off of me and shut up!" I said as I swung at him with the flashlight. Naturally, it passed right through him. It was funny how he could turn his physical presence off and on at will. Sometimes he was as solid as me, other times, he was just a whisper of an image, like a hologram from Star Wars. Joey was the strongest ghost I'd ever known and the friendliest. Most of the spirits I encountered were creepy. At least Joey was almost human.

"Aw, thank you." He smiled sweetly and glowed again. With a disgusted snort at his obvious mind reading, I slung the covers back and flicked on the flashlight. The bright light filled up the room, but I kept the beam focused on the door. One of us had to be the grown-up in this situation, and as always, that was going to be me.

Andrew? Look...I found the baby...

The ghost continued to hum and whispered her strange, heartbreaking lullaby but it didn't bring me peace at all. Not in the least. I glanced back just in time to see Joey's light flicker out and my quilt flatten as he vanished.

Great, I was all by myself and about to face off with a ghost woman and her crying baby. I wracked my brain for meditations or visualizations that would protect me. I didn't sleep with my crystals, although it felt like an oversight at the moment.

I slid out of bed as quietly as possible. Clutching the flashlight in a death grip, I reached for the doorknob. I reached slowly because I wasn't exactly sure what I planned to do.

I am a medium. I can do this. This woman needs help. I have to help her.

I can do this. I am a medium...

It wasn't much of a mantra, but it was the only thing I could drum up on short notice. Joey suddenly flickered beside me, his eyes riveted on the door. At least he wasn't shining too brightly. He had a serious expression on his face, and I glanced at him quickly before I suddenly grabbed the doorknob and snatched it open.

Immediately my flashlight failed. Either I needed new batteries, or the ghost had siphoned off the power.

Before me was a woman in white. She kind of floated, bobbing a few inches off the floor she did not touch with her feet. Her gown was voluminous, an old-fashioned type with three-quarter sleeves and lots of lace around the neck. Her hair was extraordinarily long, but the top portion of it was tied back and away from her pale face. Her hair was pitch-black, her skin glowed slightly, and she had the appearance of a young woman.

At least she wasn't bloody. There's that at least.

The spirit did not look at Joey or me, but she knew we were present. She wasn't watching us but the baby she held in her arms. I couldn't see the baby, only the white blanket it was wrapped in. She cooed at the infant who'd mercifully stopped crying. She whispered her lullaby and continued to float, bobbing up and down like she was floating on water. Her strange motion was making me seasick.

"Excuse me," I began as Joey slid back and behind me.

How did I ask her if she needed help? *How can I help you?* I asked her in my mind, but she didn't answer or indicate she heard me.

"Close the door, Chloe," Joey warned me, but I couldn't move an inch. I've never been frozen with fear before, but that was what I was experiencing at the moment. I still had the light pointed at the spirit, and to my surprise, the flashlight beam flickered on briefly. Apparently, that was the wrong move to make because her head began to turn toward me ever so slowly. I could see more than a profile view now.

We were face to face with only a few feet between us. She wasn't floating anymore, and what I saw made me want to scream my ever-loving head off.

Her face was rotting. I mean, dead-rotten. Half of it appeared decomposed, with bits of bone showing. The entirety of her face was whitish gray, and her lips were black, as were her eyes. This woman didn't want my help. She wanted something else. Without even thinking about it, a terrified scream erupted from my mouth, a loud and piercing shriek. Joey and I were screaming in unison.

Joey was jumping up and down beside me, and I instinctively tossed my flashlight at the ghost, who had begun inching toward us.

Then out of nowhere, all the lights came on, and just like that, the menacing figure vanished. The air crackled with electricity. The hallway was full of brilliant light, as was my room, although I was pretty sure I hadn't been able to turn my lamp on earlier. Someone must have been looking out for us. Thank goodness the ghostly apparition had vanished and taken her baby with her.

That's when I saw Tamara coming down the hall toward us.

What if it wasn't Tamara and it was the ghost again? Joey must've been thinking the same thing because we stepped away from the door and were still screaming when she entered my bedroom.

7

TAMARA

"What in heaven's name is going on here? What are you two doing?" My hand was on my chest as I tried to still my beating heart. It was pounding like a freight train, and I wasn't sure I was going to make it if they didn't stop screeching.

Joey and Chloe faced one another as if to ask who should tell the story, but neither one of them said a word.

"What is it? What happened?"

Joey glowed as he paced back and forth and shook his hands furiously. "It was horrible! And I do mean horrible! I told you there was a ghost in this house! Nobody ever listens to a thing I say. She keeps chasing me and calling me Andrew." He stopped his pacing and flopped down on Chloe's bed, but whatever power he had he was losing because the bed didn't move, and his luminosity began to fade.

"Would you mind telling me what's going on, Chloe, because he's not making sense. When did you get home? I didn't hear Lynn's car, and I've been here all day." I was totally confused but determined to get to the bottom of it. I felt a little guilty I wasn't in the house when whatever paranormal happening occurred. Clearly that's what was going on here because Joey never got this freaked out unless it was a supernatural event.

Chloe put her hand on her forehead and closed her eyes as if to focus. She took a deep breath and said, "All I know is I was asleep. I woke up because Miss Thing here decided to come into my room and crawl in bed with me. The power was out, my flashlight went out too, and there was a ghost lady in the hallway. She was going to charge us when the power came back on, and my room lit up."

Now was the time to confess. "I saw a woman too. The other night, she appeared as a twisting shadow in my room, and she crawled on my ceiling. I thought she would charge me, but I got away. I've been trying to communicate with her, but she's not talking to me. She seems more interested in Joey than in you or me, Chloe. You say she called you Andrew?"

"Why haven't you told us?" Joey demanded as he sat up bolt upright on the bed.

"I'm telling you now. You aren't always easy to find, Joey. I was going to tell you."

He was on a roll, though. "She had a ghost baby and it was crying. Oh my God, Tamara! It was like that Victorian up at Edward's Point. She was something straight out of a movie. Oh, the horror. Her face was all decomposing, and she called me Andrew. If you two don't mind, I've got to go lie down. Don't do any of your woo-woo stuff tonight, Chloe, because I might need to pop back in. Later!" Joey sailed out the open door and left us alone in Chloe's room.

"Are you okay? I'm sorry I wasn't here. I just stepped outside for a few minutes, and when I realized the power was off in the the house, I came right back in, and I heard you two and..."

Chloe removed the batteries from her flashlight and tossed them in the garbage can near her vanity table. "Don't worry about me, Tamara. I'm just peachy. Just seeing terrifying apparitions and whatnot, all by myself unless you include the Ghost. Situation normal. If you don't mind, I'd like to go to bed and try to get some sleep. I've got a lot of studying to do tomorrow."

"Tomorrow is Sunday. Are you telling me you were here half the day and I didn't know it? What's up, Chloe?" I didn't mean to come off as a worrywart parent, but I had a right to know where she was and why she didn't come home when I expected her to. Whether she liked it or not, I was her guardian.

"You want the truth? Because I'd really like to give you the truth." Her question surprised me, and I could tell there was something really bothering her beyond the normal. She tossed her flashlight in the nightstand drawer and slammed it shut.

I plopped down on her beanbag chair and nodded my head. "Yes, very much. I would like to hear the truth, whatever that might be. Whatever you're feeling you can tell me. I think I can handle it."

Chloe sat on the floor not far from me with her legs crossed. As terrified as she had been just a few minutes ago, she was full-on furious now. She was so angry or hurt or whatever it was that she completely forgot about the ghost woman and her baby.

Don't be a coward, Tamara. Don't cry or show weakness. You take whatever she says like a woman. She deserves that, and you can handle it.

"You forgot Mom's birthday. You forgot all about her, and you were supposed to be her best friend. I made cupcakes, and you didn't even ask. You didn't mention it or anything. It's like... It's like you're just posing, Tamara. It's like you were never my mother's friend. How could you forget her birthday?"

To my surprise, Chloe was wiping tears from her eyes, clearly broken over my decision to pretend it wasn't Tina Louise's birthday the other day.

"Oh, God, Chloe. I should've known that you would remember. Of course, I remembered your mother's birthday. She was my best friend. But if I'd had a birthday party for her, she would kick my ass. I know you and your mother had a different relationship, but as her friend, I was expected to pretend she was always twenty-five no matter how old she got. That's just how she was. We both worked in an industry that frowned upon getting older, and we didn't enjoy our birthdays because every year they rolled around was an opportunity for your agent to let you go. I did remember!"

Chloe wiped her eyes with the back of her hand and stared at me. "Seriously? But Mom is gone now. Surely, we can celebrate her if we want to. I thought you just forgot."

I crawled out of the beanbag and went to sit by her on the floor. I took her hand whether she liked it or not and squeezed it. "I'm sorry I wasn't there when you were a child, Chloe. I should've insisted Tina Louise come home more. I should have made her come back to Crystal

Springs, but I didn't know how everything was between y'all." I didn't know about you at all, I thought to myself.

"I guess it's easier to blame you because you're alive and you're here. I didn't know Mom didn't like birthdays. I made cupcakes for her, and she probably didn't even like them." Chloe laid her head on my shoulder and began to cry.

"That's nonsense. You were her child. Of course, your mother would have loved your cupcakes. She loves you still. With you, I imagine, Tina Louise didn't have to pretend she was anyone other than herself. I'm sure you celebrating her birthday is just peachy keen with her and guess what? Going forward we're going to have a party for her every year whether she likes it or not. If she has a problem with it, she can haunt me."

Chloe sniffed again. "That's just it, Tamara. She doesn't haunt me. I have Joey and these other ghosts turning up, but never Mom. Never directly. Why? I feel like she hates me or something. I don't understand!"

I held her and let her cry it out. I did not have any answers for her, but I could at least comfort her. When she got still and was cleaning her face in the bathroom, I went to her bathroom door. "Hey, come with me. I want to show you something."

"Okay?" Chloe answered as she patted her freshly washed face with a towel. She pulled her hair back in a ponytail and padded behind me as we went downstairs.

We didn't go to my bedroom but to the room I used as a storage room. It was right beside my bedroom. There wasn't much in there except for boxes of things I didn't know what to do with. It didn't take me long until I found what I was looking for. I reached over and grabbed a blanket from the cedar chest, and I spread it on the floor. I sat down on it and began to flip through the dusty scrapbook. Chloe sat beside me as I turned the pages. Each one depicted a special event and featured photos of either Tina Louise or me or both of us during a performance. There were no nude photos, just the two of us having a blast as characters from our burlesque shows. I had made this scrapbook for Chloe some time ago, but I never had the courage to give it to her. I kept turning the pages until I came to the one I was looking for.

It was Tina Louise, her bright red hair perfectly combed and her fake mole perfectly penciled on her cheek. We were born the same year, yet she always managed to look like a woman from another era. She said more than once she felt as if she had been born at the wrong time. I sighed at that memory of this photo. How quickly she came into this world and left us all wanting more. It was my turn to shed a few tears remembering my best friend. Despite the fact she kept many secrets from me I believe she loved me as best she could. I had certainly loved her, and I had never had such a friend as Tina Louise Ridaught Carol.

In this picture, her lips were perfectly painted. It was a close-up shot of her face, and in her red-gloved hands, she held a lit cupcake with white frosting and lots of sprinkles. I couldn't remember what year this was, but it felt like yesterday.

Another year, another attempt to pretend to be young.

And then she was gone.

I handed Chloe the scrapbook with a smile.

"See? It's okay to celebrate her birthday, and I'm sure she would've loved those cupcakes. Just never make the mistake of putting the wrong number of candles on her cakes." I smiled, trying to lighten the mood. Chloe clutched the scrapbook to her chest and kissed my cheek.

"This is mine to keep?" she asked sweetly.

"Today and forever," was my answer.

"Thanks, Tamara." With that, she left me in the room sitting on the floor on the blanket. I sat a little while and rummaged through a few other things, feeling extremely sentimental and sad.

I didn't have time for this. I promised Kevin I would try to reach out to that Aaron guy, and I wasn't going to achieve that here.

According to the paperwork, he had been found dead at the back of our property on the dirt road that ran behind the place. It was a way back, but I think I knew a path I could take that would lead me to that section of the road. No one used the road anymore, but it was certainly doable. I went back to my room and changed my clothes into jeans and a t-shirt, socks and tennis shoes. I pulled my wild blonde hair up on top of my head and stuffed my backpack with the equipment I would use.

Of course, I would bring the digital audio recorder and my camera, but I was also going to use my brand-new spirit box. Unlike the older version, this particular spirit box didn't focus on any one radiofrequency. It constantly ran through them all, which gave the disembodied voices more opportunities to speak to me.

I went into the kitchen to grab a few protein bars and a bottle of water when I ran into Chloe again.

"Are you going out?" she asked me point-blank.

"Yeah, I'm going to do a spirit box session by the road." There was no reason to lie to her. "Deputy Patrick, I mean Kevin, asked me to help him with a cold case. A young man died out here in the 90s. His name was Aaron. I'm trying to reach him to see if he can tell me more about his killer. They don't have any good clues. I thought I'd give it a shot and put my new ghost box to work."

"That sounds incredible! Can I go?" After our recent bonding session, I found it difficult to say no. I gave her a few minutes to change her clothing and waited for her at the bottom of the stairs. While I waited, I called out a few times for Joey, but he did not appear.

"Joey, if you are listening, I'm going to do a Periscope session. You'll want to watch."

Even that didn't entice him to step out of the wall or spring out of the dryer. He was probably still scared shitless. I was glad to see Chloe's tears dried and that we'd made up as friends. I like having Chloe as a friend. I had to remind myself she was not Tina Louise incarnate. Chloe was her own person and liked her own things and did things her own way. It was my job to mentor her and to help her have a good life but also to get to know her and let Chloe be who she needed to be.

Keys in hand, I locked the front door, and we went outside and around the house. As we walked, I shared more of the information I had gathered from the deputy, but Chloe stopped me.

"The less I know, the better. I'm working on becoming more intuitive with my gifts. What I'd like to do is to go with you and watch your session but maybe have my own session before yours just to see what I pick up. I'm not as accurate as I would like. Is that okay?"

"That sounds perfect to me. I appreciate you trying to learn about your gifts. I totally support that! Maybe you can hold the camera while I do a Periscope session for Joey. He's all into that. It's his new favorite social media platform. If I let him, he'd have his own page."

Chloe's answer was to roll her eyes. Joey was a bit over the top, but I loved him. He was my best friend.

We tried hiking straight back on the property, but it was thicker than I remembered. We had to meander a bit to avoid mucky areas. The stickers were bad too, but there were fewer gopher holes. After some work, we were at the road, and it was clear there had been no traffic here in years. The wildlife was abundant. I saw a young doe scamper off, along with a family of vocal squirrels. The foliage was infringing upon the forgotten roadway. There wasn't a house to be seen besides ours, and I could only see the tip-top of that.

"I wonder where this road leads? Do you think this is where we see the lights? Could this road be the pathway the dead use? Remember around Halloween? We kept seeing all those lights out here."

I agreed with her that it looked like the same area. From the window, it had seemed much closer. Now that we were here, and looking back at the house, it was definitely farther than my earlier assessment. To my mind, the house to the road to the abandoned barn made a sort of triangle, but it didn't look like that from the ground. What a weird effect.

I kept my thoughts to myself as Chloe began her work.

"Is anyone here? My name is Chloe, and this is Tamara." I quietly slid my digital recorder out of my pocket and hit the record button. If someone was talking to Chloe and she was unable to hear them, the recorder would catch what they were saying. It would be good to have proof for her that she was connecting even if she thought she wasn't. I'd love to see her build her confidence with this gift.

"I need to talk to Aaron. Aaron? Can you hear me?" Chloe spotted the recorder and held her hand out. I gave it to her with a silent nod. I smiled to encourage her to keep going. She began to pace up and down the road stopping every few feet to look around and stare at something I couldn't see. "You were in a car, Aaron. Do you remember?" Interesting. I never told her that. She asked a few more questions, and I played it back for her.

There was silence even in the playback, but Chloe did not let that deter her. She clicked record again and kept going. "Okay, Tamara. I'm just going to keep talking because I'm feeling and seeing things I don't understand. Maybe I will understand later."

I nodded in agreement and whispered, "Go ahead, Chloe."

"He's waiting for someone. He has dark hair, and it's slightly wavy. He put stuff in his hair to make it stick up everywhere. He thinks that's a cool style. He's got a really bad pain in his neck. I mean, it's like..." Chloe put her hand to her throat and shook her head as if she couldn't quite understand what's happening. "He can't breathe. He came here with someone, but then...oh, no."

"What is it? Don't leave me in suspense," I demanded as I watched Chloe's face turn pale.

"There is another person out here. Not Aaron, and not with Aaron. She is much older. I mean, older dead. It must be the woman looking for Andrew. She's so angry. I...I can't help her. She's out of her head, I think. She's just screaming and making no sense. Oh, God! Tamara! She wants me to die!"

"Just stop, Chloe. Stop connecting with her. Take a deep breath and have a seat on the grass. It's okay. You did great. You can't help everyone, you know. You just can't." Chloe took some deep breaths to calm herself and sat in the tall grass next to the road. I stood in front of her to observe her and protect her from the unseen. I clicked on the flashlight because the light was fading fast. It would be full-on dark out here soon. In my investigative experience, that's when the spirits got the most active, but I didn't want to put Chloe at further risk.

"Call it a night, Chloe. I think you should head back. I'll hang here and work the spirit box. Did she hurt you?" She wasn't having any of it.

"If you're staying, I am staying!" She was on her feet again.

"If you're sure. Let's try the spirit box to see if we can figure out who this is that's threatening you. Aaron was here, and you were right about the car, but this other woman interrupted. She clearly wants our attention. Let's give it to her but on our terms. If she has something hateful to say, she can say it to me." Chloe rubbed at her throat and silently agreed with me as I flipped on the spirit box.

As soon as I flipped on the machine, it began making a crackling noise. A flurry of voices came through, but there weren't any that made sense. Someone screamed. Someone laughed. A few other voices whispered to one another. I pretended it didn't creep the hell out of me.

"My name is Tamara, and this is Chloe. I'm here to speak to the lady who came to Chloe's room. How can we help you? Tell us your name. Who is Andrew?"

I heard a soft feminine voice whisper an answer. "Alice." Chloe snapped her fingers at me, and I repeated the name back to the box.

"Did you say your name is Alice?" A flurry of other voices came through, but that particular voice didn't speak again

"No!" Another feminine voice screamed through the spirit box.

In a firm voice, I said, "I want to talk to Alice and no one else. Step away from the spirit box unless your name is Alice. Alice, can you hear me?"

After a few seconds of warbled talking and scratching sounds, we heard, "Yes."

"Alice, what can we do for you? How can we help you? Have you lost Andrew?" This was Chloe now, standing on her feet. Her hands were shaking, and my heart was pumping. I don't know what we expected to hear, but it wasn't this.

Andrew...come back!

With a scream of despair, Alice was gone, and all the other voices returned. Laughing and whispering, all unhelpful voices. What did I expect? I did a ghost box session on Dead House property. Naturally, we were going to get many answers and not just one.

This one left me cold. We tried a few more times, but nobody else wanted to talk, and Alice was long gone. Poor

Aaron hadn't even come through, but at least Chloe had seen him, and we learned he had come here to meet someone. Chloe had not seen any photos of Aaron, but she had gotten his description correct. I would show her his picture later, but for now, my heart was heavy. To think someone's child had been murdered on this property. Alice must have been the woman who came to my room, too. She was seeking help, and Chloe had done such a good job of banishing ghosts from her space, at least for a little while, she came to me first. Or second. She was definitely seeking Joey.

There could be no doubt about it. The Reaper had not collected Alice. I suspected that was because Alice demanded justice for something.

Chloe and I walked home in silence.

8

TAMARA

"Boy, the camera really does put ten pounds on a person, doesn't it?" The voice over my shoulder was none other than Joey's. He finally decided to show up, and naturally, he had to have a snarky comment when it came to my appearance.

"I'm not listening to you and your negativity. I look just fine. The camera is a little off, but Chloe did her best, and I'm grateful for her help. You should have been there smarty-pants. You could have seen everything firsthand. Honestly, isn't it a bit shameful you are a ghost who's afraid of other ghosts? What does that do for your rep in the spirit world?"

My friend narrowed his eyes. "Rep? What decade is this again? Of course, I'm afraid of ghosts. We have too many crazy-ass spirits hanging around the Dead House. I blame that on Chloe and you. Any clues on this weird lady or do I need to put a pillow in the dryer and just spend the rest of my existence hiding there?"

"Her name is Alice, and she's looking for Andrew. But

I'm sure you guessed that." I smiled at his suggestion of sleeping in the dryer. Eventually, I would have to break down and fix a room up for him. I don't know why I was so fussy about it. Joey pretty much had free reign over the house now, but it was never that simple with my ghostly friend. Joey wanted his room freshly painted. He wanted shag carpet, tulip lights, and a king-size bed. God only knew for what reason. The list of his wants was long, and right now he wasn't getting any of it. If he wanted to sleep in the dryer, that was fine by me.

"Your ghostly tormentor is not the target of my investigation, but she keeps coming through. You know what they say, the squeaky wheel gets the grease. She's very squeaky, so Chloe and I will certainly have to deal with this woman before we can move on to the actual case."

Joey gasped beside me. "You have a real paranormal investigation? A real client? What? You should have told me." He clapped his hands joyfully. He was always my biggest fan, no matter what I did.

"Calm down. It's not a paranormal case, per se. I'm helping Deputy Kevin out with a cold case."

"Ugh. Can't the guy do his own work?"

I ignored his snide remark and filled him in on the details. "A young man died, and he asked me to look into it. No big deal. The only thing is, I can't seem to talk to him. When I try, I only connect with this Alice person who's screaming about Andrew."

Joey shivered, and it was a funny sight because he kind of fluttered a little. I shut down the computer and rose from the chair to stretch my back. It had a little ache in it. Sometimes it did that if I sat too long.

"You missed it, Joey. The morning after my experience I did EVP EMF work, but it was dead, pardon the phrase. Not so much as a peep."

He paced the floor, pondering what it could mean. Of course, neither of us knew the answer. I'd have to dive in a little deeper, try to do more work and see if I got lucky. That's really what paranormal research was all about. Getting lucky with evidence and getting lucky with connecting with the dead in a real and helpful way. It would be easy for a dead person to misinterpret our intentions.

That was something to consider.

In an attempt to divert his worry, I told him about our success with the new social media platform. "Check it out," I said as I powered up the computer. "Periscope is where it's at. People love my investigative videos. Especially the one from the Crystal Springs Cemetery. We have over a hundred followers already, and people want to see more. I'm thinking about making some field trips, me and Chloe, that is, to check out a few of the local hotspots. Too bad you can't come with us."

Joey peered closer at the computer screen and watched the video. As it faded to black I could see his handsome face in the reflection of the screen. He wasn't totally luminous like normal, but he was very physical-looking, almost lifelike.

"Yes! I knew it! You'll have to do more Periscope videos. Give the people what they want, and they'll love you. I want to tag along but through the videos, of course. I'm more of a homebody than you are as of late." Meaning he currently didn't have the power to leave the Ridaught Plantation if I decided to investigate off-site unless it was to pop next door to the neighbor's place. I hadn't mentioned to him the road we were investigating was out in the back of the house. I couldn't say why.

Joey was always very secretive about his abilities. I sometimes got the feeling he didn't trust me enough to tell me the whole truth. If he did trust me, he would tell me much more than I knew. For example, I didn't even know how old Joey was or his actual birthdate. I did ask questions without appearing to be too direct. I posed questions like, "What's your sign? I bet you are a Libra." But he never fell for them. He'd mock me with some smartass answer or distract me by asking me a question.

Other times I didn't think he was being coy at all. I believed he couldn't remember. At times he couldn't remember who he was or where he came from — or where he was supposed to be. When I witnessed moments like that, I felt very sorry for him.

Very sorry indeed.

Those moments never lasted. He always came back to his exuberant self, full of life. A life he could not lead because the truth of the matter was Joey is dead. There was nothing I could do to change that. The only thing I could do would be to convince him to move on, but he never wanted to talk about that. I couldn't and wouldn't force him to do it. How did I know what was waiting in the beyond? I couldn't comfort my friend and tell him I didn't know. I was too much of a friend to coerce him into leaving if he wanted to stay.

The truth of the matter was I loved Joey, and he really was my best friend. Joey followed me into the living room, and we sat on the couch together as I flicked on the television. It was still early in the evening, but there should be something good on. I needed to write my book, but I couldn't just ignore him. Joey had been absent a lot lately, and he had missed a few episodes of the new show called *Haunted in the Hereafter*. It was more like a soap opera/paranormal documentary/romance type of thing than an actual paranormal show. I was having a hard time wrapping my mind around the concept and had not really come up with an opinion about it. I wanted to like it, but it was weird.

Living people married to the dead? Cheating with the dead person? It was actually kind of gross.

Knowing Joey, he would love it. He usually loved weird shows but nothing as weird as this, so far. "What have you been doing with yourself? I hope you're not harassing Linda. Is that why you've been absent so often?" It made sense he would. Linda was next door, and he took exceptional joy at tormenting the wannabe psychic.

"Can't right now. I'm saving up my energy." Joey tucked his legs up next to him, completely ignoring the fact they were mostly missing. He always forgot to materialize his legs. I said nothing about it because it was just the two of us. "Besides, Linda is no fun anymore. She barely notices anything I do and spends her days on the phone gossiping about her husband. She's convinced he's having an affair. He's not, by the way. This show is ridiculous. Totally made up."

"I agree," I said as I changed the channel.

"I don't think Robert cares for Linda that much. They

are about to move anyway, so I'm sure you'll have new neighbors soon."

"The neighbors are moving? Why? Did you do something? What did you do? Tell me everything," I said as I put the television on mute and turned toward Joey. I could tell by the excitement on his face he was dying to give me the skinny. I wasn't prepared for the drama that was going on right next door.

"You didn't hear this from me," Joey said as he put his hand on his chest and shook his head. He looked over his shoulder to make sure no one was listening. "But Robert has a little bit of a problem. Actually, it's a big problem." Joey rubbed his fingers together to indicate money, but I wasn't sure where he was going with this. I started guessing.

"He steals money? He needs money? He's bad with money? I'm running out of answers! What? Just tell me?" I threw the remote at Joey playfully, and it passed right through him.

He frowned and said, "Ow. That was uncalled for. You are the worst at playing charades, aren't you?" He waved his fingers again, rubbing them together. "He's spending all their money. He's maxed out all of the credit cards, taken out three mortgages on the house, and he's up to his eyeballs in debt with his business. Robert or Robbie, as she calls him, is a bit of a gambler." Joey rolled his eyes and pursed his lips as he put his finger to the corner of his mouth thoughtfully. It was a silly pose, but I couldn't help but laugh.

"Seriously? They seem so...so..."

"You could dream up a million words and that would

literally not be the right word because they are all about the pretense. You know what's really funny," Joey whispered as he leaned toward me. I pretended his cold breath didn't leave me shivering. "She thinks he's hot. Can you believe that? Some people's taste."

I laughed at his description of Linda, our gossipy neighbor's, thought process. "They are husband and wife, and you're supposed to be attracted to your mate, aren't you?" I said as I drew the blanket up around my feet and legs. Our favorite show was on, but it was a rerun. I didn't want to reach through Joey's body to get the remote I'd thrown at him.

"Oh, precious. You know nothing. Absolutely nothing. Let me tell you all about it."

Apparently, Linda and Robert had been married back in the 1980s, but they got a divorce in the 1990s, but then they started living together and have continued to do so ever since. It was scandalous really because he's the deacon at the Third Baptist Church. Nobody is the wiser. Linda likes "living in sin." Joey used air quotes around that phrase. He did love his air quotes.

"How could you possibly know that? Did she tell you? Have you been revealing yourself to Linda?" I couldn't believe what I was hearing. I felt a little like Joey was cheating on me, which was proof I put too much importance on this relationship. Chloe was right. I am a weirdo.

He pulled his legs up tighter and shrugged his shoulders. "I just hear things, and I know things. It's not that big of a deal. Don't make it weird, Tamara. You know how it is. When you're with someone long enough, you pick up on things about them they would rather you didn't know." I felt my face flush at his words. Was he suggesting he...

No. I couldn't believe that. He would never spy on me like that.

He kept on rolling with the information. "She thinks it's all kind of thrilling, but Robert is a mess, girl. A big old mess. Here's another truth. Robert doesn't want to re-marry her. If he did that, Linda would know his secret—that he is completely underwater financially. Currently, Linda can't poke her nose into his business because she isn't his legal wife, and as long as he tells her what she wants to hear and her credit card works properly, he'll get away with it, but he's getting really desperate. I mean, really desperate. Like, you could see him on *48 Hours* desperate."

"Get out of here. No way is Robert dangerous. I mean, he is so diminutive."

Joey rolled his narrow green eyes. Hey, his eyes were green!

"Right, because short people don't kill anyone. Do you hear yourself?"

I didn't know what to say. That was rather naïve of me to think. Killers came in all sizes and shapes. They did not walk around with signs on them that read, "I'm a bad guy."

I chewed my lip as I pondered this unexpected bit of information.

"Do you think she's in danger, Joey? Should I tell Kevin?" I clutched the blanket tighter and stared at my luminous friend. I was getting colder by the second. Clearly my presence was making him stronger. It was a quiet thing he did that we never really talked about. He borrowed my energy a lot, and sometimes it left me really tired, other times plum sick, but I never complained. He wasn't mean about it, and he couldn't really help it. I'd have to go to bed soon, though, if he didn't stop siphoning away my natural energy.

As if he overheard my thoughts, he began to dim, and he moved away a little bit on the couch. "I'll keep an eye on those two. I don't think we have anything to worry about. Robert would rather run away from the problem than face it head-on. He's the kind of guy who likes pretending everything is fine until he finds himself buried in concrete." I shuddered at his words and quickly changed the subject. Joey complained about the re-runs, but we watched another episode.

"Sorry, Joey. There's only one *Dead Files,* and those guys are working as fast as they can to bring you good investigations. What about *Ghost Mine*? You liked that one, didn't you?"

"Meh. I could take it or leave it. You know what? You should do your own paranormal show, Tamara. We could call it *Stripper Supernatural!*"

"What?"

He jumped up and down and squealed, completely ignoring my protest. "Oh, my God! This is the best idea I have ever had! You investigate strip clubs. I'm sure those places are haunted. Just think about all the energy in those places. You need to write this stuff down." Joey began to pace the floor, waving his hands as he spewed out his unwanted brainstorming session.

"We could use the Periscope channel to build a fan base! And you could do a calendar! Like a Tamara shot a month!

This is a perfect idea because you're beautiful and you're spooky. That's like catnip to paranormal people."

"You think I'm beautiful?" I asked in a surprised voice. He'd never complimented me like that before.

"I'm dead, Tamara, but yeah. I think you're beautiful."

His excited demeanor faded quickly, as did his luminosity. I wrapped the throw blanket around me tightly. "That's the nicest thing you've ever said to me, Joey. I think you're pretty cute too."

His eyes didn't meet mine, and I got the feeling he was embarrassed by this turn of conversation. At least I'd gotten his mind off the *Stripper Supernatural* show idea. That was never going to happen.

"Do you ever think about what would have happened?" I asked quietly as I watched him glide toward me. "If we could have met in life? Would we have been friends?"

He sat on the couch again.

"What would have happened when? I can't believe you don't like my idea, Tamara. I think you should think about it. You're being really short-sighted. So you stripped a little; it's not a big deal."

"I wasn't a stripper. I was a burlesque performer. There is a big difference."

"Did you take your clothes off?" he asked as he pursed his lips disapprovingly.

"Yes, but it was all tastefully done."

"Strip-per."

"No. I didn't flaunt my body. The goal was to be seductive and playful, not pornographic. I didn't lie on the floor or do the hoochie-coochie."

"You say tomato, I say potato."

I smiled at his idiotic attempt at a comparison between the two very different performance types. "I was a burlesque performer, not a stripper."

"Fine. You were a snobby stripper. Denial for the win!"

"Have you ever wondered if we would have been friends in real life? Or would we have just ignored one another?" I asked hopefully. I wasn't sure exactly what I was asking, but I was definitely wondering what he thought.

"Oh, that. Well, I would have been a little older than you, but sure, we would have been friends."

He was stealing all the warmth, but I was careful not to fuss at him about it. "In fact, I would have swept you off your feet, Tamara." His voice dropped, and he spoke quietly, with mock seriousness. "We would have gotten married and had 2.5 children."

"Joey, give me a break."

"We would have bought a small house on the Cape of somewhere, adopted an Irish setter named Roxie, and you would have bought me a motorcycle for my birthday because I always wanted one."

Just knowing Joey would never have any of these things broke my heart, but he was definitely having me on. "Really, Joey? I would have never bought you a motorcycle, and I'm pretty sure I would not have made you happy. Not in the slightest."

"You are right. I would have cheated on you with the handyman." He smiled his silly smile, and all the seriousness of the moment vanished.

"That I believe."

"Picking on you is too easy. Uh-oh. Your crush is here.

He's walking up the steps now. Later." Joey's sad smile lingered a bit after the rest of him, like the Cheshire Cat, and then he was gone.

I went to answer the doorbell and pushed my 2.5 children out of my mind. My biological clock was ticking, and I didn't know how I felt about having kids of my own.

Why was I romanticizing motherhood?

Some questions shouldn't be asked or answered. I politely waited for the doorbell to ring and opened the door with a friendly smile. In that second, I knew the truth...Kevin Patrick was my future.

Where the hell did that come from? Get it together, Tamara.

"Hey, Kevin. Nice to see you."

"Nice to see you too. Sorry to drop in without calling, but I was in the neighborhood, and I had this six-pack..."

"Come on inside. I could use a cold one."

9

CHLOE

Tamara had company downstairs, and Joey had made himself scarce, which was a rarity. I briefly wondered what he thought about Tamara's budding romance with the cop. He must not have any objections because he wasn't acting out, flouncing up and down the hall or sighing dramatically. I opened my bedroom door and whispered his name a few times, but he didn't appear. He told me it bothered him when I treated him like a genie in a lamp.

"I am not Beetlejuice, Chloe. You can't summon me by saying my name a bunch of times. Igmo. All you'll do is annoy me, and trust me, you don't want that."

Of course, then I made fun of him for saying the word "igmo" and his ability to get annoyed so easily. "Does it bother you I can manipulate you so easily?"

He answered by sticking out his ghostly tongue. I asked Joey what year he was born, what generation he claimed. Was he a generation Xer? "Clearly a better generation than yours."

There was neither hide nor hair of the resident ghost

tonight. I guess he had better things to do, like make the chandelier swirl around. I wasn't sure that was anything other than Joey messing with us.

The family home felt very still as if the air was waiting for something to emerge, or we were on the verge of some huge manifestation, but I had no evidence to support that feeling. It was so like me to drum up problems when there weren't any. Would I ever learn just to be happy in the moment? I walked down the hall quietly and checked in all of the rooms to make sure I truly was alone up here.

First room? Check.

Second room? Check.

I continued to make my rounds and was happy to verify there were no phantoms hiding in any of the dusty corners or closets. There was no sign of the Reaper. I could also verify there were no weird sounds of clanging chains or stomping feet. Not that I'd ever heard clanging chains here at the Ridaught Plantation, but I certainly wouldn't rule it out.

Anything was possible in this place.

"Okay. So we're good." I wasn't sure who I was talking to, but it felt good to say it like some sort of proclamation. I paused in the doorway outside my bedroom and wondered what to do on this exciting Sunday night. I had already ransacked the remainder of my mother's trunks and recovered everything I thought was useful. I even told Tamara about it to let her know it was me rooting around up there and not some ghost.

To my surprise, she was very understanding about the whole thing, and I adored the scrapbook she gave me. Tamara totally supported me, but she'd reminded me that

Mom was human and if I happened to find items I might deem questionable to have a little mercy. I wasn't sure what she was talking about at first, but then her meaning dawned on me. That had been a weird conversation.

"Are you talking about weed pipes? Or other freaky stuff I don't want to know about?" I grilled Tamara, but she just smiled and shook her head.

"I have no idea what's in your mother's things. I'm just saying. We weren't born old ladies. We were young women, and we made some goofy mistakes from time to time. You have seen some of our costumes." Tamara made a face, and I couldn't help but laugh. "Even your mother, as sophisticated as she was later in life, was once an angsty teenager."

Naturally I had to re-examine all of her trunks to make sure I didn't miss anything crucial, but there wasn't anything illicit or illegal amongst my mother's treasures. Her gowns were stored in my closet now, as well as her shoes, which were unfortunately a little too small for me. But they were pretty to look at, and I liked having them around.

I decided to give my friend Lynn a call to see what she was up to. Her cell phone went right to the automated message. I wasn't sure what her house phone number was, but I probably wouldn't have called it anyway. Her father was a monster and one I didn't want to encounter again, even by phone if I didn't have to. I thought about calling Trey, not for any romantic reason, but just to find out if Lynn was okay. I was pretty much over him and had the sneaking suspicion he had moved on from me.

Trey lived next door to Lynn, and he could get a

message to her if she was grounded or something. She was probably grounded for something ridiculous, as always.

Where was Lynn's mother? Did anyone care about what was going on over there? I did, and I was going to do something about it. As I reached for the phone, I nearly jumped off the bed because it began to ring. I picked it up and saw Trey's name on the screen.

That was a little weird. I was just thinking about him.

"Hello? Trey?" I walked to the window just to have something to look at as we talked. How was I going to play this? Did I really want to see him again? I wasn't sure. I had been so enamored with him when I first met him. Trey seemed like the total package, but now I was getting a whole other vibe, and it had to do with that car. Too bad I didn't have time travel skills. I'd love to go back in time and set that thing on fire before he ever received it.

"Hey, what are you doing?" I hated Trey's stupid conversation openers. Couldn't he think of anything more interesting to say?

"What am I doing? I'm talking to you. Hey, I'm kind of glad you called. I've been worried about your cousin. How is Lynn? Did her father ever go back on the road? Did your dad come home?"

Those cousins had the worst parents. It was like that family was cursed or something. I shivered just thinking about it. Yes, definitely a curse. I should trust my intuition on this one, and my intuition was telling me they were certainly cursed, but by who?

"That's a lot of questions, Chloe. Let me try to answer them all. I haven't seen Lynn. I haven't seen my dad. And yeah, I think Jack's back on the road. But I'm calling about me and you, if that's okay. I was hoping we could get together. You know, chill like we used to." His voice had that smooth sound to it like he was trying to be sexy.

Before I thought about it, the words just came flying out of my mouth. "What about Vanessa?"

"What about her?"

"I thought you liked her. I mean, I haven't heard from you in forever, and then you just call me out of the blue? I saw you with Vanessa in the hallway. The way you two were acting, I thought you liked her." The memory of Trey touching Vanessa's dark hair and smiling down at her inspired jealous thoughts. Thoughts I did not welcome and were not natural to me. I didn't like being a jealous person. I wasn't a game player, not in the slightest. I never wanted to be with someone who brought that out in me because...

As Trey stammered and sputtered on the other end of the line, I stared out the window and hoped he could put together a decent explanation for what he was doing with the other girl. He wasn't doing a great job at the moment. In fact, his whole ambiance was putting off a "I'm guilty" vibe.

That's when I saw the small amber-colored lights. They seemed to follow one another in a strange pattern about three feet off the ground. They hovered in the air but were moving of one accord. Strangely enough, not toward the house but away from it. They were headed to the dirt road behind my family home.

Trey was still talking, but I wasn't paying much attention. I was too focused on the entities moving down the pathway. I felt troubled, and I felt so many things, but none of them was patient. "Do whatever you want, Trey. I've got to go."

I hung up the phone and tossed it on the bed. Could it be Alice trying to reach out again? How could I help her? Maybe I should just leave her to the Reaper?

From the conversation downstairs, Tamara's soft laughter and the deputy's deep voice, those two were getting along well. I didn't want to mess that up. I had a new softness for Tamara, a new respect and appreciation for her. If she could find happiness with this deputy guy, I was all for it.

Besides, I liked being on my own, which was probably why I wasn't overly concerned about Trey. I was still quite concerned about Lynn, though. I'd have to do something about that situation even if it meant sticking my nose where it didn't belong. Lynn may resent me, but I was her friend, and I couldn't allow her to get mistreated without saying anything to Tamara or at least the school guidance counselor.

For now, Alice needed my help. If I was going to become a decent medium, I needed to practice my skills. I remembered the basics, visualizing the light, seeing the door, opening the door. It was true Tamara had guided me through the process at first, but it now seemed so simple and intuitive. There was no time like the present. I reached into my nightstand to get my flashlight. I replaced the batteries and verified it was working properly.

I slid it in my pocket. I left my phone behind because I didn't want to be interrupted by Trey's nonsense. I could've put the phone on silent, but just knowing I had it with me felt as if it would break the spell. I went with that and decided to head out of the house as quietly as possible.

It was easier to go out the back door as Tamara and Kevin were hanging out in the living room. It wasn't completely black out. The stars were shining, and there was a half-moon above me. The grass in the backyard was getting far too high. One of these days, Tamara and I would have to cut it just to keep the snakes and vermin away from the house. I'd found a snakeskin in the attic not long ago. That's not what you want to see in your home.

I eased out the back door quietly. Tamara had soft music playing in the kitchen window. She did love her old radio and left it playing all the time. All the lower floor windows were still open from earlier today. It had been nice to allow fresh air to blow into the place. I'd meant to do that on my floor, too, but forgot.

"Alice? Is that you?" I could no longer see the tiny amber-colored lights, but I sensed I was not alone out here in the yard. Using the flashlight, I walked carefully away from the house and into the grassy depths of the backyard. I had almost made it to the back of the property where the road was when suddenly Joey was there.

"What are you doing, Chloe?"

"I'm trying to give Tamara and Kevin a little privacy. It would be nice if you did the same. I'm just checking something out," I said, trying to ignore his eyes. He could always see right through me, not to mention read my mind. It was a bit unsettling.

"I saw those lights too. You're not fooling me, Chloe Carol. There is a ghost in the house already, and the

Reaper is out here. You know what that means! Why must you poke the bees' nest?"

I caught my breath at hearing his revelation. "Stop it. Are you serious? No dramatics. Where have you seen the Reaper? Out here?" I stared at Joey, who thankfully wasn't currently glowing like a lightning bug. He looked as real as anyone, except for his feet. He always got his feet wrong. At least he was better at manifesting legs now. Where did he get all this energy? That question and so many more made me suspicious of him. Joey shook his shaggy head sadly.

"Still don't trust me? Fine. Go talk to the ghosts, Chloe. Don't come running to me if they don't want to let you go. I'm telling you the truth. The Reaper is out here, and he's coming for someone. I'm not ready to go." With that, Joey began to fade and walk away.

"For Pete's sake! Stop reading my mind. It's really wrong and unfair. I trust you, you big pain in the ass. If you want to come with me, fine. I'm going to talk to Alice. If I can help her move on, I want to do that."

Joey brightened slightly and said, "I don't trust her. I'm telling you, she's not all there. Being dead can make a person crazy, and this Alice chick is definitely crazy. We should wait for Tamara. There needs to be more than just me and you out here."

"Tamara is not a medium, Joey. And if I don't practice, I'm never going to get better. I'm never going to be able to put these spirits to rest. Isn't that what you want? What we all want? I have to practice." I shrugged my shoulders and waved my flashlight around in frustration.

It made perfect sense to me, and evidently I got through

to him because he sighed and said, "Fine. Let's practice. But if the Reaper shows up, you're on your own. I'm not ready to cross over yet. You can't force me, you know."

"Is that what you think? I would force you to cross over? First of all, I don't even think that's a possibility. From what I understand, spirits have to be willing to move into the light. Second of all, whether I understand it or not or like it, you are my friend. I would never do that." My voice sounded softer than I expected, and I meant the words which made Joey glow a little brighter. "But tone down your light. We don't want every...

Suddenly, I saw a young man standing behind Joey. The same young man I'd seen yesterday when Tamara and I were out working our spirit box session. He couldn't have been dead for very long because he was modern looking but not alive. No. Not alive at all. Before he turned to face the intruder, I saw Joey's expression shift. His eyebrows narrowed as if he sensed the spirit's presence.

The stranger had a handsome face with dark wavy hair, and he was about Joey's height. The ghost was muscular but somewhat thin. He wore blue jeans and a t-shirt with an open plaid shirt over it and a leather necklace. He had a tattoo on one of his hands. I couldn't read it, but it was definitely a word.

"Who are you? I asked instinctively.

As if he didn't hear me, the ghost walked past Joey and me in a few seconds and disappeared into the foliage beyond us. On the other side of the greenery was the dirt road. That's where the amber lights had been heading.

As I turned my attention back to Joey, his expression broke my heart. His hand went to his mouth, and he gasped as he sobbed once. I had seen a true ghost, and one thing was clear.

Joey had seen him too. By his dimming luminosity, I could see he was devastated. Recognition flickered across his face. "Joey? What is it? Do you know him? Talk to me." His response was another sob, and then he vanished like someone turned him off like a light switch.

Waving my flashlight around, I realized I was alone in the field, and the thought disturbed me greatly. I heard tree limbs breaking just beyond my vision, but there was no evidence of anyone walking around.

I didn't know what to do. I had to check on Joey. I had to go back to the house and tell Tamara, even if it pissed her off.

The ghost lights were gone, and the cracking wood sounds had ceased too. I was definitely on my own out here and feeling very vulnerable.

I took off running back to the house.

TAMARA

I was dragging this morning. Chloe had asked me about Joey last night but was elusive about her concern. I surmised she did not want to talk openly about him in front of Kevin. Following her lead, I slipped out of the room to give us some privacy, but other than a few moist tears in her eyes, she didn't have anything to tell me.

I hadn't seen him, and I told her that. She asked me again this morning, but I didn't get a chance to question her further because I had a visitor. I'd barely tossed a blueberry muffin into Chloe's hand when I spotted Kevin coming up the steps of the back porch. We'd had a great time last night and hung out for hours, but I didn't expect him to show up early this morning. Wasn't he going to be worried about what the neighbors said? Apparently, Linda kept her eyes on this place.

"You need me to pick you up, Chloe?" I shouted at her as she headed to the bus.

"No. I'll probably catch a ride with Lynn. Later." She waved at me without glancing back and climbed on the bus as if she owned it. I definitely saw a change in attitude. She hated riding the bus, or at least she used to. I guess once you faced down ghosts and whatnot, punk kids weren't anything to be worried about.

I tucked my hair behind my ear and smiled at Kevin. I was sure I looked like a train wreck, but this is what you got when you showed up for unexpected visits. "What brings you to my neck of the woods so early in the morning?"

A strange squeaking sound interrupted us, and I held up my finger. "Hold on a second." I walked out of the kitchen and down the hall to try and track down the weird sound. Above me, the chandelier was swinging, practically rocking back and forth. The hair on my arms stood up, and I heard Kevin catch his breath behind me.

"Are we having an earthquake?" I asked.

"Hey! Stand back. If that comes down, it could kill you!" I stared at the thing as it began to wobble slightly. Was Kevin right and the chandelier was about to hit the ground? I could barely process what I was seeing when I heard a groaning sound coming from the room upstairs directly above where the chandelier hung. It wasn't an occupied room. Chloe and Lynn used the room sometimes to goof around in, but as far as I knew, it was just an open room with no furniture in it. Kevin looked at me, and I looked at him without saying a word. We both traveled the perimeter of the room and headed up the stairs. There was only one way to find out what was happening, and that was to go right to the source.

As we pounded up the steps, I detected another sound, a familiar growl like the one the Reaper made when he used to visit this place. Oh, great. That's all I need.

At least Kevin would be here to witness whatever was about to happen. We both walked down the hall into the room that was over the chandelier. There wasn't anything out of place. There was no furniture to speak of except for a lone dresser, and the light above us was nothing remarkable, just one of those cheap plastic shades that covered a light bulb.

"It's been happening, and I can't explain it unless there's some kind of seismic activity, but why wouldn't it make other things move around?" I looked at the deputy to see if he had any more answers than I did. He didn't.

"I haven't heard anything about a seismic event. We don't even get point-ones here. I mean, if it was a gravel truck or some kind of construction happening nearby, then yeah. But there's nothing like that that I know of, and I think I would know." Kevin got down on his knees and pressed around the center of the floor with his hands. I guessed he was looking for soft spots, but I didn't see any, and neither did he. He sat up and shrugged.

I snapped my fingers. "Let's do an experiment. I'll go downstairs and watch while you stomp around up here, and let's compare notes. Maybe somehow the flooring is causing the chandelier to bump around."

"Look at you, getting me involved in all your investigation stuff. Okay, let's give it a try. Yell at me when you get there. But remember, don't get underneath it. I'm serious. That thing must weigh a hundred pounds. If it falls, it's going to smash whatever's beneath it." I frowned as I walked out of the room.

"Thanks for the vote of confidence," I said as I headed down the stairs. Strangely enough, when I got there, the chandelier was still. It was as if it had never moved in the first place. "Okay? I'm down here, and it's not moving. Give it a shot!" I could hear Kevin's footsteps and his muffled reply, but nothing happened. That chandelier didn't move at all. It sure wasn't rocking back and forth as if it was a drunken sailor. "Nothing! Try it again! Do it harder!"

"I'm giving it my best. Are you telling me it's not moving an inch?" Kevin shouted down to me.

"Not an inch. I can't explain it!" I called back loudly.

Kevin joined me at the bottom of the stairs and we both looked at the chandelier, but there was nothing else to see. Whatever had triggered the activity had stopped. Just for laughs and giggles, I opened the front door and slammed it. Nothing. Apparently, Kevin was thinking along the same lines because he headed into the kitchen and slammed the back door. Nothing happened. We couldn't make the chandelier swing to save our lives.

"I guess the best thing to do is to get a professional in here to look at it. Just to be on the safe side," he suggested as he helped himself to a cup of coffee. I smiled and didn't say anything when he began ransacking the cabinets for coffee mugs. I finally put him out of his misery and opened the cabinet right next to the coffee maker. Some detective, I laughed to myself.

"Do you happen to know any?" I asked as I handed him the sugar bowl and took a seat at the kitchen table.

"Yeah, actually I do. One of the guys I work with, his son is a master electrician. His name is Mike. Young guy but pretty reliable. Want me to give you his number?" he asked as he poured way too much sugar into his coffee.

"Yes, please do. Not that I'm not glad you're here drinking up my coffee and using way too much sugar. But surely there was a reason why you came by so early?" Before a girl had a chance to dress up a little, I thought. My hands nervously went to my wild blonde hair.

He flashed that lazy grin of his, and I suspected he wanted to say something flirtatious but refrained. I was beginning to like the friendlier side of Deputy Kevin Patrick. Who would have believed it?

"What is going on with the chandelier is a bit of a puzzle. After you told me about the ghost of Alice, I remembered an old news story. A shocking murder from back in the day, and I do mean way back in the day." He pulled a folded piece of paper out of his back pocket and slid it toward me. "This is a copy of an old newspaper article. It was easy enough to find. I stopped by the library this morning."

I raised my eyebrows. "How early does the library open? It's not even 9 AM yet."

"One of the perks of the badge," he said proudly as he sipped his coffee. I snickered but unfolded the paper and began reading the article.

"Mrs. Alice Loper. It says she died here with her daughter. Possible murder?" It was a horrific piece describing a horrible murder scene. "Did Mr. Loper confess? What could possibly have been the reason for such a heinous act?"

Kevin drank his coffee and set the mug to the side. "That's the weird thing. I understand they kept records a bit differently back in those days, but there is absolutely nothing in the public record to explain any of it. I found one interview sheet, and there was a note. Mr. Loper told the sheriff he didn't hurt his wife, but she'd been unstable for a while. Except for that night, he had no memory of what happened. Supposedly Mr. Loper said as soon as he left the property that day, he couldn't recall anything. It was like he had some sort of amnesia."

I slid my hand on the table in shock. "Are you serious? Could it be Mr. Loper got away with murdering his family? That's unbelievable. I get the feeling Alice Loper wants us to know the truth. She desperately wants us to know something. I also get the feeling I'm never going to be able to reach Aaron if I don't help Alice first. Some ghosts are louder than others, stronger, and she is very strong."

Kevin tilted his head as he studied me. What was he thinking? I had no idea and I didn't ask, but my heart broke for Alice Loper and her kids. "Just the two girls? That's all she had? Did they both die?"

"Yes, two girls. One of the Loper girls got away. She was injured, and she recovered. Her name was Annabel. Unfortunately, she was very young, and there's no record of what she may have seen or witnessed, if anything."

I twisted my lips as I thought about what he said. "Wait. Annabel lived? What was the other child's name?"

"Annabel and Betsy. Betsy, the youngest, died. They were found on the second floor. Right where..."

I finished his sentence for him. "The chandelier hangs. Ugh. So they were all found together in that room? I think it used to be a nursery." I wasn't asking a question really, just talking out loud. We sat in silence for a moment. I had to give Deputy Patrick props for not calling me crazy. At least he was willing to accept what was happening here at the notorious Dead House, and obviously he thought I could help him somehow. I decided to change the subject to something more familiar. I could ponder the chandelier activity by myself later. Maybe I could get Joey to help me do some investigating.

Yeah, right. Not likely.

"Thanks for this. I'll review it and see if I can talk to her later. Maybe I'll read it out loud and see if she responds. By the way, how is Sheriff Jarvis feeling these days? Any improvement in his condition? I know chemo can be hard on a person."

Kevin's worried expression clued me in on the real situation, but like any true friend, he held out hope for the sheriff. "The man is a fighter, in every sense of the word. I better go. My shift starts in thirty minutes. I just wanted to bring that to you." Kevin glanced at his watch and rose from the table, and I followed him.

"Thanks for bringing this by. I'll dive into more research, and please send me the number for the electrician. You said his name was Mike, right?" With a quick glance down the hall toward my room, I led Kevin to the door. I could feel an unearthly chill in the air, the kind of chill that often accompanied Joey's ghostly self. Kevin didn't stick around for more than a few minutes.

I chit-chatted with him on his way to the vehicle, and he hovered outside his car for a few seconds like an uncertain teenager. I was no mind reader, but I definitely got a might-want-to-kiss-me vibe. I wasn't going to make this easy. I waved goodbye and headed back inside.

Always leave them on a high note. I couldn't help but smile to myself.

I quickly tidied up my hair, grabbed another cup of coffee, and headed to my office. I was feeling inspired this morning. I could see in my mind's eye how the first scene should begin.

The beginning of a book was always my favorite part of the process. I powered up the computer, opened a fresh document, and typed in a title I was sure I would change at some point. Diving right into the scene, I let the characters take me where they wanted to go.

This character, the main ghost in my story, was making a tragic mistake. He was trusting the wrong man. "It's not polite to read over someone's shoulder, Joey." He didn't have a witty answer.

I turned to speak to him. "What's wrong, Joey? I can see it all over your face."

Joey smiled, but it wasn't his normal luminous beam. "Are you two getting serious? What's up with that, Tamara?" He changed the subject again.

"We're just being friendly. I'm helping him with something. Now make yourself scarce for a few minutes. I need to get some words on the page."

"Fine, but that's really not flowing, is it? How about doing something about my stalker? She's everywhere, Tamara! Crying and bleeding...it's disgusting!"

He vanished before my eyes. "Joey?"

"I'm here, just conserving energy for tonight's movie marathon. It's the Director's Cut for *Howlers*. Don't tell me you forgot?"

"No, I haven't forgotten," I lied. "But have you noticed

anything weird going on with the chandelier? Are you playing with it?"

Joey didn't answer me right away. Had he left? "Joey?"

"I'm here, just thinking. That's her old room, I think. I stay away from that area nowadays. She's always moaning and crying, and the Reaper is getting closer to the house. He wants her, I think."

"I think our ghost is Alice Loper, a lady who lived here a long time ago. She died upstairs, along with one of her children. She never got justice. For a long time, people said she killed her child, but it's very possible her husband murdered her and he got away with it. I don't understand the connection to the chandelier. Just be careful, will you?"

"Stop giving me the creeps, Tamara Garvey. Ugh, I'm outta here for a while. Later."

Then he was gone. I didn't even get a chance to talk to him about Aaron or anything. How quickly my excitement for writing became frustration. I was a big ball of tangled irritation now. I closed the computer and decided to go outside for a walk. It was a fine morning with lots of warm sunshine. I slung my hands in my jeans' pockets and continued to walk the path that led to the road.

The road where Aaron had been found so long ago. There were too many damn ghosts on this property.

The truth was, I wasn't sure how this story would go. I was writing by the seat of my pants, and by doing so, I wasn't giving the ghosts what they needed. They needed their authentic voices to be heard. This was all supposition. I had to dig deeper. If I was going to help Kevin with Aaron, I needed Alice to step out of the way first. For that, she must cross over. How could I assist Alice, and could I do it on my own?

I didn't know, but I had a strange kind of peace about me. My inner voice reminded me to be patient and quiet. All I had to do was wait because the answer would come soon enough. That's all.

Watch and wait.

CHLOE

I did not see my face in my locker mirror. I could hear my classmates behind me, feet shuffling, pushing, nudging me out of the way. The bell was about to ring. I'd be late for class if I didn't get a move on. But what could I do except stare at the ghost of Alice Loper?

Clutching my book bag, I half-heartedly heaved it up on my shoulder. I surveyed the horrific scene that unfurled before me. What a terrible, bloody sight.

I ignored the whispers of the students that swarmed around me. "She's such a weirdo." They had no idea just how weird I was, but after the Halloween party, this should not have been a mystery to them. No doubt Chloe Carol was a strange bird, but I wasn't the only strange bird on this campus. Not by a long shot.

I moaned as I tried to turn away, but I couldn't blink or move or even speak. Forces demanded I witness the death of Alice Loper right here in my locker mirror. That wasn't something one saw every day.

I blinked a few times, but the images did not dissipate. I could plainly see Alice Loper, a small woman with a plain face. Her voluminous black hair had collapsed from her usually neat bun. The strands were caked with blood, and she had fallen against a windowless wall, holding the body of a small child. It was as if the child had been laid on her lap. Her hands weren't holding her. Tears streamed down Alice's face.

Was that a kid? Damn it! Why did it have to be a kid?

The child was not moving, and if I had to guess, the child had been dead for quite some time. The little girl appeared stiff and immovable, like an old-fashioned porcelain doll. She was a lovely, macabre little thing with her dark curls.

I sensed there were others on the other side of the mirror, just beyond. More dead that I could not see, but they could all see me and they all wanted to talk to me.

I could not stop staring. Suddenly a man stepped into view. He was much closer to me than poor Alice, and he was blatantly grimacing at me. He had light brown hair, dark brown eyes, and a furry brown mustache. *What is your name?* I demanded, but no answer came. He growled to express his disapproval of my witnessing the scene.

Too bad. I see you, you bastard! Killers don't like being watched, but I see you.

He was so close to the mirror, I was suddenly afraid he would reach through and grab me. With a bit of a scream, I instinctively slammed the locker door on him. Everyone around me paused as if they'd heard his growl too. Maybe it had been my scream or the repercussion from the slamming locker that shocked them all.

I didn't know what I'd say if I were questioned. There's a dead man in my locker, a horrible man who threatened me even though he's been dead for a hundred years.

I did not offer an explanation to the students around me. Thankfully, there were no teachers present, so I didn't feel compelled to explain my strange behavior. I didn't have the book I needed for my next class, but there was no way I was going back into that locker right now. It was my lunch break, but I had no appetite. I hadn't even eaten the blueberry muffin Tamara handed me on my way out of the house. I gave it to a kid on the bus, Ross something or other. I guess I could choke down a soda if the machine wasn't empty again. The vending machines in this school sucked. What teenager drinks diet soda? Maybe by the time lunch was over, I would have the courage to reopen my locker.

Maybe Lynn would help me. She had the same lunch break as me, and she was easy to spot with her shiny blue hair. The color had faded some, but her eye makeup was ridiculously dark. Lynn's personal style was always evolving. Unfortunately, so was her taste in friends. Two of the goth girls were camped out around the table with her, and they were whispering together when I walked up.

"Hey," I said to all three of them. "Got a minute?" That last comment was directed to Lynn.

To my surprise, Lynn shrugged her shoulders as if she weren't sure how much time she could allot to me, her occasional best friend.

"Excuse me, Spooky, but Lynn is in the middle of a reading. You'll have to come back. Now go be dark and brooding somewhere else." Allison or whatever her name had turned her back to me and held her palm out to Lynn. My friend glanced up at me without so much as a shrug. She immediately began staring at Allison's open palm as if she could truly discern clues about Allison's future there.

"No, excuse you, Allison. I was talking to Lynn, not you. As I said, do you have a minute?" I shifted my heavy book bag back up on my shoulder. Why was this thing always trying to slide off? Probably because I always overloaded it with way too many books and notebooks and pens and all my crystals. Might as well stuff my friendship with Lynn in there too because apparently, that was good and broken.

She rolled her eyes. "Yeah, sure. Be back in a sec, Ally." She climbed out of the lunch table bench and walked with me to the vending machine.

"What's that about, Lynn? Are we not friends anymore? Are you embarrassed by me? That's pretty crappy considering what we've been through recently." I didn't want to openly bring her father up, but how could she be so blasé with me?

"Stop being dramatic. I'm just trying to hone my skills. You aren't the only one who sees things from time to time. Surely you don't begrudge me giving it a shot?" She bounced a few quarters in the machine and banged on the diet soda button.

"Giving what a shot? Are you suggesting that I'm keeping you from whatever this is? When did you start claiming to be a palm reader? When did that start, Lynn? I would never stop you from trying anything, but I've been worried about you and your dad."

She turned her back to the cafeteria. "Hey! Keep your

voice down!" Lynn looked back and smiled at Allison and then scowled at me. "I don't want the whole world to know what a loser my dad is, and if you're my friend, you'll keep your mouth shut about it." Lynn set her thin lips and popped her soda can open.

"You need to tell someone the truth about him before he does something terrible. Believe me, I've seen terrible, Lynn. There's a dark presence in your house, and I'm afraid it's going to hurt you. It follows you and Trey and your father." I didn't mean to raise my voice or share any of this, but the tension was rising between us.

She sipped her soda and backed away from me. "That's bullshit. And here I thought you were my friend, Chloe Carol. Apparently, I was wrong. Friends don't gossip about each other."

"I haven't been gossiping about anyone. I'm genuinely concerned for you, and something just happened I thought I could talk to you about. But you know what, you go hang out with your new pal Allison, and I'll just figure out my problems by myself. I'm pretty used to that by now."

Lynn's expression was the proof I needed to understand I had crossed some sort of line with her. I was hurt by her behavior, but that did not give me permission to hurt other people. Especially my best friend. She stormed away from me and back to the lunchroom. Again, the people around me watched it all. Allison spotted the exchange and quickly led Lynn out to the concourse.

I guess that was that then.

I got my own can of soda and sat outside until my next class. I dug in my bag, opened a notebook, and grabbed a bag of pencils. I began to sketch the scene in the locker mirror. I wasn't great at sketching, but I wanted to get the image down as best I could. I'd show Tamara later. At least she'd be interested.

The bell rang, reminding me class was beginning, but I decided to stay put. It wasn't like anyone would miss me, not really. I wondered where Trey was. He had lunch after me, but I didn't see him. From my viewpoint in the outside dining area, I didn't see either of his cars. Not his old one or the new, classic obsession. On a whim, I sent him a text, but all I got back was, **Later**.

Wow. How was I supposed to interpret that nonsense?

Later? Hardly.

Forget it, I sent back.

I wouldn't be available later. Not to anyone. I hung out in the sunshine until the buses started rolling in. I wasted no time getting on board and hurried to the back to continue working on my sketch. As always, the drive home took forever, but at least nobody bothered me. The two sisters, also teenagers, my biggest tormentors, had thankfully moved across town and didn't attend Crystal Springs High School anymore. According to some whispers right after their transfer, they'd gotten in trouble with the law. They got caught shoplifting at a local department store.

As my bus pulled up to my stop, I shoved all my stuff back in my bag, and I dragged the heavier book bag with me. I felt as if I was carrying the weight of the world. What was I going to do about Lynn? I felt I had to tell someone. She really could be in danger. How else could I explain her change in personality?

I could hear Tamara's radio blaring in the kitchen and smell food cooking. Even though I felt as if we'd made up somewhat, I didn't want to burden her with all my concerns. Instead, I shouted, "Hey!" as I climbed the steps and raced to my room. I opened the door and tossed the bookbag in the chair. Joey was already there. He was sitting cross-legged on the floor. He patted the seat beside him, and I wasted no time collapsing there.

To my surprise, I cried. I wailed, actually, like a big old baby. Tamara's music continued to rock the kitchen, so she didn't hear me. I was glad for that. I couldn't face her right now.

Joey lay on the floor beside me. He kindly didn't touch me since his hands always dropped my body temperature, but he smiled. It was a winsome smile.

Winsome. I like that. What does that mean exactly?

Hell if I know.

That was Joey's voice in my head. I didn't normally like having long conversations with him in this way, but at the moment, I found it quite comforting.

He smiled again. *It means charming, I think. Even I know that, and vocabulary wasn't my strong suit back in the day.*

I let the tears flow, but at least I wasn't bawling like a kid now.

There are worse things, Chloe. He's too dark for you, trust me. He's too dark. And she's not much better.

"What do you mean?" I asked him as I wiped my nose with the back of my sleeve.

Gross. Those two are following in their family's footsteps. What can I say? The apple doesn't fall far from the tree. They are cursed, and they are all in their curse together. They choose to be cursed, whereas you don't have a choice. Neither did your mom.

"So it's true. Mom is being blocked from coming to me. Like a curse?"

No, not like *a curse. It* is *a curse. You are cursed.*

She couldn't be here with me, no matter what. I felt so desperate I reached out and cautiously touched his face. I don't know why, I guess because I just needed a friend. A real friend.

"Just this one time, Joey. Help me reach out to Mom just this one time. I will never ask again. I promise. I know you can do it. I need this." He wasn't very luminous, but his expression conveyed his understanding. Another tear fell, and it dripped on the carpet beneath me. I let it flow and reached out to Joey again. I knew his skin would be chilly, but he very kindly manifested himself like a real human. Like a living person.

Part of my brain screamed at me, "Think about what you're doing, Chloe! You're asking him to push past the curse. Don't do this to him!" He heard my thoughts and knew my mind and put me at ease.

I will do it. I think that's why I'm here. I need to make this right for you and then maybe... Let's try, shall we? I can do this.

He closed his eyes and, following his lead, I closed mine. In our shared mental space, I could see what Joey was doing. He was focusing on a dull spot on the black wall before us. It was a wall of darkness.

Joey, what am I looking at?

Hush...and focus.

I heard him whisper my mother's name. *Tina Louise. Your daughter is here. She needs to talk to you.*

Slowly the dull spot began to look like an erasure mark. A kind of smudge. We had managed to remove some of the darkness. I couldn't say how Joey was working against the darkness, and all I could think to do was focus on manifesting light. A bright, white light, like the kind I used when the dead needed to cross over. My whole body tensed, and I hurt from my head to my toes, but I stared at the spot and willed it to brighten and show what was hidden from me.

A woman's face briefly appeared before me, blocking my view of the wall of blackness. With a nasty scowl, she screamed at me in a language I did not understand.

Alice? Go away! There was another woman too, another ancestor of mine. They were related, but I couldn't quite catch her name. *Please move aside! I need to talk to my mother!*

I whispered Joey's name to make sure he was okay, and that he was still with me. He squeezed my hand, and strangely enough, it didn't feel cold. It was as if we were both ghosts. Two ghosts with cold hands. If I died, then it is what it is. I needed this. I need to talk to Mom.

Don't think negatively, Chloe. Not now! Focus on the spot. Look for Tina Louise. I don't know how long I can hold her back. She's a...oh, God, she's a witch!

Who? Alice?

Focus! Joey screamed at me.

I caught my breath and continued to focus on the wall. I used all of my abilities to visualize the light with all of my strength. To my surprise, the darkness began to fracture and it became brittle, like paint chips, and flakes of black crumbled and fell to the floor.

Joey moaned beside me and I could sense he was

wrestling with the woman, my ancestor who wanted me to leave this place for good. As he twisted and grunted, she began changing shape. Her arms and legs vanished, and she became a snakelike creature. The woman turned herself into a snake, and a shrieking Joey was working hard to prevent her from snapping at him with her fangs. With a renewed sense of purpose and fear, I walked closer to the wall. Large chunks of the barrier were gone, and I became keenly aware there were others. Not like Alice or the snake thing but other spirits, and soon they would see the wall was down. I had to move quickly, think fast, and find Mom.

As I felt the sting of tears in my eyes, I spotted a woman to my far right. I saw her red hair. She was not far away, still on the other side, kind of frozen like a sculpture or a wax figure. Then her glittery green eyes moved. She was aware of me! She saw me, and with her awareness of me, she became animated—not a thing of wax, not an image but my mother!

Mom? It's me, Chloe. Mom? Can you see me?

Mom smiled at me briefly, but then her smile vanished.

No, Chloe. You cannot be here. It's not safe for you. Not at all. You have to leave. Please, go. This is a place for the dead. She keeps us all here. Annabel...

I sobbed as Joey swore at my left. The snake with the woman's voice was getting the best of him and threatening to drag him into the darkness on the other side of the crumbled wall. The woman's scream shook my soul and filled me with fear.

Please, Mom. I need you. Come back with me. Together we can break the curse, and then you can come home. Please...Mom.

I reached past the wall, ignoring the painful shock wave that struck me. It felt like a strong electrical current. It not only hurt but filled my mouth with a bad taste. Mom wasn't strong enough to pass through the wall, but if I could continue tearing it down, continue reaching for her, she would be free. She could do it if she just tried! She should be free. Always and forever! I suddenly became aware of Joey struggling.

Maybe I could bring her back to the house. Dead people liked our family home. Why shouldn't Mom come back with me?

Joey screamed as the snake thing came toward me. His voice echoed in my mind. *No, Chloe! You can't bring her back! No one can come back! Just you! Just you!*

What do you mean, just me? You're here! Mom can come back! Mom belongs with me!

The air shuddered a bit, and I could hear the chandelier tinkling. That was funny. I was nowhere near the chandelier. I was with Joey. We were in my room, but we came for Mom. There was the wall of blackness and dozens of people on the other side. The crack, the gap, it was becoming a problem because the dead she kept there saw it. No! Not them, just Mom!

I found you! I found you, Mom!

I love you, Clovie.

How long had it been since I'd heard that name? Only Mom would know that name, my nickname. I'd always had trouble pronouncing Chloe when I was little, so Clovie stuck for a while. Mom's sparkling red hair and shiny eyes began to darken like she was a character in a noir movie, all black and white. Things were changing, Mom was fading, and the wall was reassembling around my extended arm. I couldn't stop reaching for her.

Oh, it hurt! It hurt so bad!

Mom, please! Take my hand!

You have to go back. Take her back, Joey. Please...go!

No!

MRS. LOPER

Someone wheezed beside me, and it was an atrocious sound. Was that my child? No, it couldn't be. Annabel was gone, and Betsy was in my lap. Why was I on the floor?

I'd come down the hall to check on the children; that was the last thing I remembered. I thought I heard the girls crying. I could not find Anita. She was supposed to tend to the children during my absence. I suspected she had snuck out and abandoned her post at my children's side but to leave them sick in their beds? Would she leave me as well?

That would not be tolerated. I couldn't understand. She had been a faithful servant until now. I would have to ask Mr. Loper to speak with her, that was for certain.

I was in the nursery, but I didn't know why. My girls should be sleeping in their beds. How did I get here? Betsy was in my lap, asleep, and not moving at all. Such a good girl. Yes, of the two of them, Betsy was the better behaved. Only time would tell how long that would last. The room was dark, but I could see through the window a crease of daylight breaking through the darkness. It wouldn't be long before the sun was full up, and maybe then I could move. Maybe then I would be able to breathe.

It was me wheezing and struggling to breathe. Was I dying? My head hurt so badly.

I detected the faint aroma of cigarette smoke. I struggled but managed to lift my bobbing head. Had I fallen with the child in my arms? Then I saw his face in front of me.

"Mr. Loper, help me. Andrew..."

I imagined I was screaming, but I could not hear my voice. Betsy did not stir, and she felt so heavy. As daylight began to fill the room, I could see something disturbing.

Blood on the floor and on my hands. Blood was all over me. Why could I not speak?

Andrew's expression worried me. He was sad, so very sad. *How long have you been here? Help me!*

I could only think the words, not speak them. Mr. Loper had shed his jacket and was wearing only his pants, suspenders, and undershirt. He had always been a tidy man, so it was surprising now to see him half-covered in dirt. As if he had fallen into and crawled out of a very deep hole. Without a word to me, he reached down and took Betsy from my arms. He was weeping and crying. She was dead. He laid her on her bed as I struggled to make my legs work. I didn't know how I had become so broken.

Unwanted memories flooded my mind. I was on a ladder, a rope around my neck, Anita crying out beneath me...

"Annabel? Where is Annabel?" Mr. Loper demanded, but I could not answer him.

Andrew had returned too late to save his daughters. Too late to save them. I could not recall.

Remember yourself, Mrs. Loper. Keep your wits about you. It's not too late. Oh, but it was.

Some strange resonance deep in my soul assured me of that. It was far too late after all. Andrew was back, and the bedroom door was closed behind him. He had something in his hands. A short stick, like a club. He clutched rags too. He was crying and mumbling, but I could make no sense of it. He rubbed his mustache and peered into my eyes. There was an emptiness in his. He was a lost man, and I had done this to him. Was he weeping for me?

It was then I realized I had never loved Andrew Loper. Not like I'd hoped I would when I stole him from my sister.

"Where is Annabel? I can forgive you for everything but not her. Tell me where she is? What have you done to yourself, Lavinia?" He sobbed with heartbreak. "You are broken, all broken. Let me help you, I think I can set some of those bones."

Mr. Loper continued to weep, but before I could summon a protest, I felt a solid blow to my arm. A whack of the most painful sort. The shock of being physically struck by my husband rendered me speechless, but I was already speechless because of my face. What had he done to my face? My jaw, he broke my jaw. Was he going to kill me now? No. Not him! It had been me! Why was he calling me Lavinia? I was Alice! Now and forever!

The creaking of the rope...the tinkling of the chandelier...Anita's screaming...the children crying. Yes, that had happened. All of that. Not a dream.

With my hand raised, I tried to fend off further abuse.

He did not touch me again, but he was so close I could smell his sweaty body. Andrew grabbed my leg and pressed another piece of wood to my skin. The pain was so intense it sickened me. I moaned in agony.

Let me die! That's all I want! I want to die!

He sobbed and wiped the blood off my face. He studied my jaw and probed with his fingers. "Why did you do this? Why?" Heavy tears fell on my face. I was lying on my back and staring at the brightly painted ceiling of my daughters' nursery.

You killed me, Andrew. You know who I am, and I could not live with that. You killed me, I whispered, but my tongue was too heavy, and there was blood in my mouth. If I could not swallow soon, I would drown in it, but I could not swallow.

Andrew, I think...

My eyes closed.

I could hear Annabel crying, and as I left my body, I finally found her hiding in the closet inside the hatbox. Smart, clever girl.

Annabel, you must avenge me. You must...I am leaving you my precious possession...take it...

Then there was nothing. Nothing at all.

———

"Joey! Where are you? Oh, God! What have I done?" I picked myself up off the rug and hurried out of my room. Tamara was in her office, pounding on her laptop keyboard. She immediately stopped what she was doing and spun around in her chair. The lingering effects of the vision left me feeling sick and discombobulated. It was a struggle to stand upright, as if Alice Loper had left a little of her pain with me. Or maybe this was guilt. I should feel guilty for what I put Joey through.

"Chloe? What's the matter? What is it?"

I sagged into the only other chair in her office and began telling her the whole horrible story. Tamara had neat stacks of paper on her desk, and her bulletin board was loaded with pictures and maps. I saw the photo of Andrew Loper amongst them.

A very old photo.

"That's him! Andrew!"

Looking at it made me shudder. I cried of course, but I plowed on and bared my soul to Tamara. I told her about the locker incident and seeing Andrew's menacing face staring back at me. I regretfully told her about Joey and how I asked him to assist me in reaching out to Mom, practically forcing him to do it. I told her about the vision of Alice Loper being found by her husband and her last words to Annabel.

"Chloe, your mother? Oh, God! She's trapped? Why would anyone want to keep you apart? That's horrible?"

Wait, when did Tamara start wearing glasses?

"I don't know! I really don't know! I'm not worried about a curse right now. It's Joey! I don't think he came back with me, Tamara. He said only one of us could come back. He was fighting with the witch. She changed into a big snake, but she had this horrible face, and she wanted to destroy us both. I can't believe this. I am so sorry. I'll never forgive myself."

She handed me a few tissues from her box and wheeled

her desk chair close to me. "Stop, Chloe. Don't blame your-self. I'm sure Joey is okay. He always comes out on top. I mean, he's Joey. He'll find his way home, and this is his home. We are his family. Don't beat yourself up. I swear it will be okay."

As if to defy her attempts at comforting me, we heard a strange whirring, an odd squeaking sound. "Are you hearing that?" Tamara asked as she removed her glasses and tossed them on her desk. We followed the sound, and it led us to the front room. The massive light fixture above us swirled and swung as if it would fall at any moment.

"I remembered now! Alice and Lavinia were twin sisters. One killed the other, and it's not clear who did what to whom. Mrs. Loper was mad, quite mad! I am not sure she even knew anymore. She called herself Alice, but she was really Lavinia, her sister. Maybe. She was so crazy. Oh, God. I can see it all in my mind. Her mind is so clut-tered. She thinks she's possessed by her dead sister's spirit. She was up on a ladder. Tamara! I think she tried to kill herself, but it didn't go right. It didn't go right at all."

Tamara had no chance to answer me. I grabbed her hand and took off running as the chandelier crashed to the floor a few feet away from us. Shards of glass scattered around our feet, and the house went entirely still as we held one another.

Alice or Andrew had just tried to kill us.

13

TAMARA

"Thanks for coming over, Kevin. As you can see, the chandelier is a goner, and to be honest, I thought Chloe and I were goners too. We were in the room when it fell."

Chloe was holding my hand and agreeing with me. "We heard the chandelier swinging, making some sort of weird sound, and when we came in here, it was swirling around."

Kevin squatted next to the massive light fixture and examined the wiring. "It looks pretty old, but not old enough to come down on you. You're right, you are very lucky. I'm glad you weren't hurt. I don't see any cuts or anything that would make me believe this was deliberate. So, was it moving around like before?"

I nodded my head, and Chloe agreed with me again. "It was weird. It was spinning. I know what you're thinking. I mean, I've heard the chandelier tinkle when a heavy truck went by or there was a boom in the house. But other things would move too if that was the case. That didn't happen in this instance. The chandelier was the only thing moving, and I think I know..."

"I saw it swinging too the other day. I want you both to know you can trust me."

Chloe agreed to tell what she knew but refused to talk in the front room. "At least let's go to the living room. There's glass everywhere. We're going to have to call someone in, Tamara. What do you want to bet the chandelier damaged the floor?"

We hunkered down in the living room, just the three of us. Kevin had no one with him, and I was grateful for that. It would be hard to explain all this to an unbeliever. Chloe began with her experience at school and even took the time to describe Andrew Loper. She left out a few parts, about the snake and the curse, but Kevin got the idea. "Just to be clear this Joey person, this ghost, he's the one you guys know. He's the friendly one."

"Yes, he's like a member of the family. We love Joey. I want to help him, but I think the only way to do that is to move Alice on. From what I saw in my vision, she tried to hang herself. Alice Loper was not murdered. She tried to commit suicide!"

"From what I saw, Anita fled that night because of Alice's madness. Betsy died from the fever, and Annabel was hiding. They couldn't convict Mr. Loper because he didn't kill his wife. There's a lot more to the story, though." As Chloe went on, we began to hear sounds above us. A woman's footsteps tapping back and forth, pacing the floor. I could feel her anxiety even though I couldn't hear the ghost's voice.

Kevin cocked his eyes up at the ceiling and said in a loud voice, "You need to come down here! No goofing off up there!"

I frowned at him and said, "What are you doing? Why don't you just skip on up there and tell me what you see? It's a ghost. It's probably Alice Loper. I'm game if you're game."

Kevin put his hand out as if to steady me. "Whoa. I'm not saying I doubt you or I don't believe Chloe, but that doesn't mean I'm willing to abandon my style of investigation. I thought the goal here was to work together, the three of us? Paranormal investigator, medium, and cop."

"Sounds fine by me. You're an investigator, and she's an investigator. I'm the medium. Let's go up there and confront the woman. Just a warning though, if she's tossing down chandeliers and trying to kill us, she doesn't want her secrets known. She doesn't want us here, and she doesn't want to leave. Come on, Mister Deputy. Get those handcuffs ready." We both ignored Chloe's mocking tone but obediently followed her out of the room and around the mess of glass and brass scattered across the front room. We quietly hiked up the stairs, nobody talking.

It was dead silent at the Dead House.

That didn't mean we were alone. My fingers felt sticky as if they were covered with spider webs. It was not a sensation I enjoyed. I rubbed at them and tried to remove the invisible webs from my fingers.

"Who is that?" Kevin whispered beside me. The familiar hooded figure hovered at the end of the hallway. The Reaper had arrived, which could only mean one thing. He was here to collect someone.

"Nobody you want to mess with. Don't make eye contact. Follow me. Let's get out of here, Chloe. I think we should go to the nursery."

I glanced over my shoulder, but the Reaper wasn't making any moves toward us. God, what a horrible sight. Although I could not see the eyes of the hooded figure, he was watching every move we made. I got the feeling he expected a soul. That was his job. Where I got those ideas, I wasn't sure, but I knew them like I knew my own name. He had no personality. There was nothing human about him. Like the Ferryman of old, he was merely doing his job. I shivered again and hurried into the nursery. If we were going to make contact with Mrs. Loper, this would be the place to do it. Even though we suspected Mrs. Loper or whoever she was had tried to commit suicide by hanging from the chandelier, she had died in this room. Presumably after her husband came home and found her downstairs. He had to have carried her up here. Chloe was right. There was no way she could have done the deed by herself. Technically all she would need was a rope and a ladder, but she wasn't a strong woman and couldn't have held the ladder by herself, could she?

Kevin was perplexed by what he saw. There was still the one dresser against the wall, and the closet door was open. There wasn't much in the way of storage in here either except for a few boxes. Kevin pulled his big flashlight off his belt and began examining the inside of the closet. I don't know what he thought he was going to find, but whatever it was, it did not present itself. There were no secret doors, no hidden cubbies. Whoever was walking around in this room, which we had all clearly heard, they had left.

We stepped back into the hallway to check the other rooms. There wasn't a soul in the place, not even Joey.

Thankfully the Reaper was gone. Make that invisible; he wasn't gone. He still expected to receive his prize, and we could not disappoint him. I kept these thoughts to myself so as not to alarm my investigative partners. Not that Chloe probably didn't know already.

We went back into the old nursery. Chloe began her appraisal in a very diplomatic tone, "Okay, boys and girls. This is the room that would be over the living room. We heard the footsteps traveling from this room to that room, but as you can see, there is nobody at all. Chandeliers are falling down, and we are hearing footsteps, and even you saw that entity at the end of the hallway."

"She's right. You have to admit there's nobody up here, Kevin. I think we should move on to the next step. Are you ready?" The last question was for Chloe.

"Yes, I think so. And sooner rather than later before I chicken out. Do you think this will bring Joey back?" She twisted the edge of her shirt nervously.

"I'm not sure, but it's worth a shot, and we don't have any choice now that it's here." I assumed everyone understood who it was I was talking about. I was loath to use his name again. Talking too frequently about entities such as the Reaper often made them stronger.

"What are you two talking about? What's the next step?"

I took his hand. It was my turn to calm him. "Now Chloe does her work. She's going to call Mrs. Loper out and help her move on. We have to. She's not going to go quietly, I suspect, but we have help. She's supposed to be gone. It isn't right for her to be here. Being dead and hanging around isn't making her saner. It's making her crazier."

"And we want Joey back," Chloe said to no one in particular. "I'm ready."

Kevin shook his head at this whole idea. "I've never done anything like this, and I'm not sure how much help I'll be. What should I do? Should I go downstairs and wait?" That last question wasn't really a question, but I wasn't going to let him off so easy.

"I think it's best if you're here with us. We all need to stay together. Just watch and learn. You're right. I'm not sure how much help you'll be, but this is your chance to see how we do things."

"Are we supposed to have equipment? That's what I've always seen. I've watched one or two of those paranormal shows. And your Periscope. I watch that too," Kevin confessed as he eyed the space around us nervously.

I couldn't help but smile despite the horrible situation we found ourselves in. "Really?"

"Focus, people. I need y'all to be quiet." Chloe stood in the middle of the room and waved us away. I stood next to Kevin and tried to represent calm. The truth of the matter was these types of transitions were not always easy. How was he going to react when and if Mrs. Loper came through? We were about to find out. Talk about a trial by fire.

"Mrs. Loper? You destroyed my chandelier. You have no right to do that. Mrs. Loper? Why are you here?" Chloe's head was down slightly, and her eyes were closed. She was breathing deeply, a practice she'd developed in recent weeks that appeared to help her focus her energy.

Nothing happened. We heard not a footstep, and no floor creaked. There was nothing at all. After a few attempts, I suggested we use the ghost box. I had experienced quite a bit of luck with reaching out to the dead with such tools. It was true many times the voices that came across the radio were tricksters, the dead and other entities who wanted to play pranks, but more often than not, sincere people came through and spoke.

Maybe Mrs. Loper was too weak to speak the way Chloe was used to. It did take a lot of energy to cast a chandelier down to the floor, and both of us had witnessed how erratically the thing was moving before it crashed.

"I'm open to that. I'll stay here and continue to try reaching out. I think she knows what we're up to, and she doesn't want to go."

Kevin snorted. "Well, that's too bad. I'll stay here, but you should be careful near that glass."

"Right," I said as I sprinted out of the room down the stairs and into my room. I thought I had left the spirit box in my closet with the rest of the equipment, but it was not in my closet. It was sitting on my bed, black and shiny with silver dials.

"Joey? Are you here? Please tell me you're okay. Did you get this out for me?" There was no sign of my ghostly best friend. I got the spider web feelings again—the creepy ones that threatened to bind me. The Reaper was close. So close, and so willing to take whatever soul he could with him. I raced out of my room as if I had jet packs on my tennis shoes. This was not the way I'd expected to spend my day but if we could find some resolution and put this destructive spirit to rest, life would certainly be better for all of us.

You can't go there. Just focus on the moment, I thought. I raced up the stairs and joined Chloe and Kevin in the room. She was pacing while Kevin leaned against the wall, observing nonchalantly.

He was shaking in his boots. At least he had a good game face, I gave him that. I flicked on the spirit box and put it on the floor in front of Chloe. I tinkered with the dials until I found a good setting and the right volume. We didn't want it so loud it scared the hell out of us, but then again, we didn't want it so low we couldn't hear anything. It was always difficult to find a happy medium. Every situation had its challenges.

"My name is Tamara, and I'm here to talk with you. This is Chloe and Kevin. We want to talk to the person responsible for breaking the chandelier."

An eruption of sounds burst from the spirit box. Crackling, hissing, the typical things one would experience with a radio-based voice box. It was as if everyone wanted to talk. There was more than one ghost here at the Dead House.

Kevin's nonchalance quickly vanished as he asked, "Did you hear that?" Chloe and I both shot him a quizzical look. What did he think was going to happen?

After a few seconds of listening to the static, I twisted one of the knobs and put it back on the floor. As soon as I set it down, I heard a familiar voice say, "Hey, y'all!" I couldn't help but clap my hands and grin at Chloe. It was Joey!

"I can hear you. Joey? I hear you! Are you okay?" Chloe was pounding him with questions, but we didn't hear him again. The voices called in on one another once more. A woman with a raspy voice, a whining child, and maybe a male voice.

"Is Mrs. Loper here? We need to talk to Mrs. Loper. Do you prefer Alice or Lavinia?" More erratic noise but nothing coherent. "Joey, if you are here, can you point Mrs. Loper toward the microphone? It's right here on this box." I heard his voice once more, but it was garbled. He wasn't happy. Then a second voice came through.

Not Alice!

"Not Alice?" I glanced at Chloe, but she was not giving me any clues.

"Lavinia? Is this Lavinia?"

Yes...killed me...

"I saw what happened to you, Mrs. Loper. Andrew did not kill you." Chloe's combative answer earned her a scratch. "Hell! Am I bleeding on my back? I think she just clawed me." I pulled up her shirt discreetly, and sure enough, saw a red welt rising up on her skin. This wasn't good. Not good at all.

I barked at the invisible. "Hey, you aren't allowed to hurt people! You can't touch us, Mrs. Loper! Lavinia! We are only trying to help you. That's all we want to do." I put Chloe's shirt down and whispered to her. "You're going to have to slow down with her. She can't remember, or she doesn't want to remember. Either way, this is going to be tricky."

Suddenly, Chloe dug in her jacket pocket and pulled out her charm bracelet. It was loaded with hematite, a stone that supposedly weakened negative forces. This woman, the dead Mrs. Loper, was definitely a negative force.

"Got it." Chloe clutched her beads and began again. "You were hurt really badly, weren't you, Mrs. Loper?"

Hurt.

More static and a scream. Kevin swore beside me, but he remained in place.

My head hurts. Betsy... The last bit crackled off.

"Betsy had a fever, Mrs. Loper. She died from a fever. You didn't hurt her, and neither did your husband. She was sick, Mrs. Loper."

My Annie...

"Yes, I know about Annie, but I am here to help you. Just you, Mrs. Loper."

Kevin had been doing a great job of being quiet until he was violently pushed. "What the hell was that?"

"What happened?" I asked stupidly. "I mean, what did you feel? Anything? Hands? Coldness? Dizziness?"

"I thought I saw a man standing beside me, about my height, maybe a little shorter. I turned to get a better look, and I got shoved from the other side."

"Let's gather up," Chloe suggested as she held out her hands to us. "It's Mr. Loper. He thinks you're a threat. He's just trying to protect his family."

Kevin shook his hands as he rubbed his side. "His wife hung herself, and he thinks *I'm* a threat?"

"Have some sympathy, Kevin. They are stuck in their own kind of hell. Hey, that's it! I know why she won't pass on." Chloe's eyes widened as her new awareness led her to close her eyes again. The spirit box continued to crackle and random voices came through, but none of them made sense.

"Mrs. Loper, I know you're afraid, but your husband is here with you. He hasn't left you. He never left you. He forgives you, Lavinia."

No! I'm not... Crackle and a dull humming sound that lasted for at least five seconds.

"You do forgive her, don't you, Mr. Loper? I know you do." To my surprise, a male voice echoed through the box.

Yes. Lavinia.

"Do you hear that? He forgives you, Mrs. Loper. He is right here, and he is inviting you to come with him. I'm going to open a door for you, Mrs. Loper. It's okay."

Andrew...

"That's right, Mrs. Loper. Andrew is waiting by the door." Chloe dropped her voice and asked me to turn off the spirit box. I obediently agreed and was glad for it. It was completely quiet, but we weren't alone. The air crackled with activity.

"See the light, Mrs. Loper? You don't have to be afraid of it. It is soft and warm, and inside of it, you will find Andrew. He's there, and he's waiting with Betsy and Annabel."

Kevin's hand tensed in my own, but I did not dare open my eyes. I was too busy trying to visualize a door, trying in my limited way to help Chloe lead the dead woman through the darkness and into the light.

"No one here judges you, Mrs. Loper. Even your husband forgives you. Can you see him? He's wearing the blue suit that you like. Yes, it is the suit he wore when you got married. Andrew brought you flowers that day. Tiny white flowers, like baby's breath. You pressed them in a book, but you lost the book." Chloe paused to listen to Mrs. Loper. Clearly, they were having a conversation with one another. Kevin twisted slightly, but he did not let go of our hands. I guessed he was being touched again.

"Yes, I will look for it, Mrs. Loper. I promise I will search high and low." Chloe sniffed, and I peeked at her. Tears were flowing, not the terrified kind but the kind that promised healing. "She's going," she said softly. "See the door now? There's Andrew! He's there, and he has flowers. He has those soft white flowers you love so much. Go to him, Mrs. Loper. Go with him, Lavinia. It's okay." As we listened to Chloe whisper and cry, the house shook one last time.

Then everything went still.

14

TAMARA

Days went by and then a full week, and everything was quiet at the Ridaught Plantation. Chloe appeared happier, but we both missed Joey something fierce. I knew she felt responsible for what happened, for Joey's moving on or whatever had occurred. I reminded her no one ever made Joey do anything he didn't want to do.

Never.

We picked up the pieces and carried on as best we could. I couldn't bring myself to believe I'd seen the end of him. Kevin spent quite a bit of time working. One of his fellow deputies had come down with the flu, so he took double shifts for a few days. I suspected he was trying to put some distance between us, but when I showed up with lunch one afternoon, he appeared very happy to see me. I got a chance to meet Willie Mae and a few of the others who worked at the substation.

He was supposed to show up tonight with a few beers. I grilled chicken breasts, and Chloe made a tasty salad to go with our dinner. I was glad to hear she and Lynn had made up, and although I didn't get the details, I was certain Chloe had stood up for herself. Whatever happened between them, they both needed to love and respect one another, just like Tina Louise and me.

Maybe that wasn't a great comparison, considering all the secrets my late best friend had, but I loved her still, and she'd loved me enough to trust me with her greatest treasure, her daughter.

Angelina Webster, a curse breaker from Mobile, Alabama, was set to arrive next week, and I was feeling kind of nervous about it. I'd never worked with a curse breaker before. However, she came highly recommended by more than one friend in the paranormal field. She couldn't be worse than Quentin. Like everything else here at the Dead House, we would take things one day at a time.

Kevin arrived on time, and after a quick conversation and an even faster meal, Chloe disappeared upstairs to do her homework. She never mentioned Trey anymore, so I suspected they had broken up. She was much more grounded than she used to be, and for that I was grateful.

After supper, there was a lull in the conversation. I felt as if Kevin had something he wanted to say but didn't have the courage. It was a beautiful night, and I'd been itching to go back to the road and try again to make contact with the young man who'd died back there. Now was as good a time as any. If possible, I wanted to keep Chloe out of this particular investigation. She'd been through enough. I wanted to give her some time to get over what she'd been through.

I barely got the suggestion out of my mouth when Kevin said, "Let's go. But let's not record it for Periscope. If this kid actually comes through, I wouldn't want his family to hear anything. It would hurt them. He's got a sister. I talked to her just the other day. You understand, right?"

"That goes without saying. I would never want to bring Aaron's family more hurt. Let's see if maybe he can help us solve the mystery of his murder." I squeezed his hand and kissed his cheek. I was feeling particularly affectionate tonight. Deputy Kevin Patrick better look out.

"I've seen firsthand that those voices are the best witnesses."

With narrowed eyes, I answered. "Ghosts. They are dead people, not just voices on the wind, Kevin. I agree with you, but if we can get a clue as to what Aaron might have seen or experienced, I'm sure it will be helpful."

He shrugged noncommittally but he didn't argue with me. "Should I help with the dishes?"

"The dishes can wait. It's supposed to rain later, and I'd like to get out to the road before there's water everywhere. Let me grab my spirit box."

Kevin nodded as he moved the dishes to the sink. I liked this domestic side of him. That could prove useful in the future. Washing dishes was not my favorite thing, but I found that I had to do it quite frequently even when it was just me in the house. I couldn't quite bring myself to load the dishwasher for just one or two people.

"Why don't we take my vehicle back there? The road is not in good condition, but it might be helpful, especially if it rains. Using that box in a more contained area is better, but it's better than nothing."

I hollered up to Chloe to tell her we were stepping out of the house for a few minutes, and she hollered back.

Luckily, she didn't ask questions because I didn't want her to tag along. For more than one reason.

To reach the road, we had to go down the driveway and take a right, make a half loop, and come up behind the house. It was strange to think that all of this property used to belong to the original tract. It was a lot of land. We rode in silence as Kevin did his best to dodge potholes and unseen dips in the road. We went about halfway down the property line, and he put the car in park. It was a pleasant evening although clouds were gathering. We still had quite a bit of moonlight. I wasn't sure how long it would last, but I was anxious to get out of the car and get to work.

"Ready?" I asked as I leaned against the front of his vehicle. I placed the spirit box on the hood, careful not to scratch the paint. "I'm about to crank her up."

Kevin shivered slightly but nodded as if to say go for it. I flipped the switch on and tinkered with the volume until I got it at a decent level. That didn't prevent the occasional scream from launching out of the speaker, but anything I could do to make it easier to hear the voices helped. Luckily this particular brand of spirit box allowed me to record my sessions on a digital file I could examine later on my computer. There was something thrilling about seeing those wave files in graph form. People didn't understand how easy it was to record the disembodied voices. If they did know, I'm sure it would be a world-changer for many.

"Aaron? Aaron Knight? Are you here?" We got an immediate response.

Yes!

Without thinking about it, I smacked Kevin on the arm.

This was exciting. I couldn't be sure this was the person we were looking for, so I pressed a little harder.

"Aaron, this is Deputy Patrick, and my name is Tamara. We are investigating your death. I know that's a tough subject to talk about, but if you could help us, we can help you. Aaron? Are you there?"

No.

I'm here.

Car. Dead.

"What the hell?" Kevin asked as he stepped away from the box. "How many dead people are around here?"

I raised my hand to remind him to be calm. "I can tell there are a lot of you out here, but I need to speak to Aaron. Aaron, do you know what happened to you? Can we talk about it?"

Joey...

A young man's voice came through, and it was not Joey.

"What about Joey? Did you come here to meet him? Was he your friend?" A sudden burst of desperation rose within me. It was true then, Aaron and Joey were connected. Somehow, I'd known that from the get-go. I wondered if that was why Joey had been so standoffish.

"Aaron? This is Deputy Patrick. I'm investigating your case. Do you know who killed you?"

There was silence, and then a sudden burst of energy hit the box and manifested in a strange way. A song began to play, a familiar song by Simply Red.

The desperate voice came over the speaker again, the same young man.

Joey?

"That's impossible. This radio has no antenna. It can't

pick up songs like that. Pieces of songs, snippets of voices, but not play an entire song. This is crazy." I turned up the volume slightly, and a cacophony of voices came through. The young man's voice whispered something, and then there was a deeper voice, one that sounded almost inhuman. Until that moment, I hadn't thought about the Reaper, but could this be his voice? As far as I knew, he didn't speak. He did like to appear menacing and enjoyed staring and growling but not speaking.

Help...Joey...

I turned the spirit box off. I couldn't take it anymore. I rubbed my eyes and refused to let the tears fall. It was clear to me this dead young man was worried about his friend, worried about Joey. He didn't know he was gone and didn't understand Joey was gone, too. Suddenly, Kevin's arms were wrapped around me. A light sprinkling of rain cast across Kevin's jacket and my bare arms.

"The bottom is about to fall out. We better get in the vehicle." I didn't argue with him. I was ready for this session to be over and quite frankly had chills all over my body. I suspected that we had made contact with Aaron, but he was not going to be able to help us. He was too disconnected and confused to be of much help, like many murder victims.

Kevin slid his keys into the ignition and the interior lights came on, but I put my hand on his. "No, let's stay here for a minute. Just a minute." I forced back the tears, and before I knew it, his lips were on mine. He kissed me, and I kissed him right back. A few minutes into our delightfully agonizing make out session, I whispered in his ear, "You better take me home before there's no going back."

He whispered back, "We are way past that point, Tamara Garvey."

"I agree," I said breathlessly. "Way past. So, what are we going to do about it?" As he drew back to remove his jacket, I kicked off my shoes and slid into the back seat. It had been a long time since I'd been in the back of a police car, and certainly never willingly. Kevin was too muscular to heave himself over the seat without knocking me unconscious. He turned on the radio softly and eased into the backseat via the door. I scooted over to make room for him.

"Are we breaking the law?" I teased him.

His warm hand stroked my cheek confidently. "We are two private citizens on private property having a private conversation. That's my story. What's yours?"

I touched his lip with my finger softly. I enjoyed those lips. I was excited about the possibility of exploring the rest of him. "Are you looking to write a report?"

Deputy Patrick unbuttoned his shirt and tossed it over the seat. I mimicked his movements, sat confidently on the backseat of his vehicle, and waited for his answer. "No, ma'am. I plan on being a first-hand witness."

"Sounds good," I answered as he pressed against me and we collapsed onto the seat. The rain began to fall, and the music played softly. It felt right to be in the backseat with Kevin. Completely right. I didn't think too much about the horrible things that had happened on this road, the sad, wretched things that occurred on the Ridaught property. I thought about this moment and this moment alone. I needed to get lost in him, lost in us.

We managed to steam up the car in only a few minutes. As we careened into mutual satisfaction, I rubbed his neck with my hand and he kissed my ear softly.

To our surprise, the spirit box kicked on. All by itself.

Joey? Are you there?

15

TAMARA

As Kevin's vehicle pulled away from the Ridaught Plantation, I stepped inside the house after saying goodbye with a quick wave. Talk about bad timing. I definitely came in at the wrong moment. The two teenagers, Chloe and Lynn, were lumbering down the staircase with empty chip bags and soda cans. Obviously, they were coming to the kitchen for refills and were laughing and giggling until they saw me.

At least those two were getting along again. I was happy about that. Not so much about getting busted trying to sneak back inside, looking like I'd been rolling around in the backseat of a car.

I suddenly wondered what my ponytail looked like. I hadn't given it much thought since climbing out of the back of the police car. It was probably all jacked up, but if I reached for it now, I would definitely appear guilty. Showing any kind of weakness when you're parenting a teenager was a bad idea. Even I knew that.

"Whatcha doing?" Chloe asked as she crossed her arms

and leaned against the wall. She wore a smart-ass smile that stretched across her pretty face. Funny how she looked like her mother right then.

"Oh, just working on an investigation with the deputy. Doing some work." Lynn snorted beside her, but Chloe elbowed her into silence. I worked on keeping my face blank as I shoved my hands in my pockets.

Oh, shoot. Why were my pockets hanging out?

Chloe's grin deepened. "What kind of investigation? Anything we should know about? Lynn and I are up for anything. We're kind of bored, actually. We might watch one more movie before she goes home, but we've got time. So, what kind of investigating are you doing again?"

I shook my head and tried to look cool. "The paranormal kind. What other kind is there? Now, if you'll excuse me, I'm going to go put this spirit box back where it belongs."

They sputtered and giggled behind my back, but I ignored them. I was sure my face turned fifty shades of red, but it wasn't until I cleared the hallway mirror that I saw what they were giggling about. My hair was definitely jacked up, and my t-shirt was on backward. My pockets hung out like I'd been robbed.

No, I didn't look guilty at all. To be fair, it's not like we hadn't gotten dressed in a hurry. The spirit box had come on by itself, and it freaked us both out and put a damper on the mood. For a fact, Kevin was weirded out. I sighed before my reflection when Chloe stood behind me, shaking her head. "I'm sure I don't want to know how your investigation went down."

"Hey, cut that out. Guilty as charged, but can we

change the subject? I think I'm going to turn in early tonight. Please do a better job than me of staying out of trouble."

She hugged my neck and tugged at my lopsided ponytail. "It's okay to be human, Aunt Tamara."

I froze in my tracks. She'd never called me that before, and I intentionally didn't mention it. Best not to make a big deal out of it. Aunt Tamara. I liked that nickname, and it had been her idea.

"Hey, quick question. Are you going to be around tomorrow? Do you have to work?"

"Not until tomorrow evening. Why? What's up?"

"I'd like your help with the spirit box. As I mentioned, I was with Kevin tonight, and we were working with the spirit box when Aaron's voice came through. I turned it off, but it switched back on by itself. Aaron really wants to talk. He's looking for Joey."

"I figured that. I should have said something to you. I think they knew one another."

"Really? Aaron keeps asking about him. I hate to even ask you to do this after the Loper thing, but do you feel up to helping me connect with him? We'd really like to get to the bottom of his murder. Sheriff Jarvis isn't well, and solving these cold cases is kind of important to him."

"Whatever I can do for Joey or you, of course I'll help." Chloe hugged me tight, and I hugged her back. "Now go get a shower. You smell like a cop who wears too much cologne."

I laughed before I finished the walk of shame down the hall. I went to my bedroom and closed the door behind me. The girls had the radio on in the kitchen. I liked that; not necessarily their choice in music, but I liked having music playing in the house.

Aunt Tamara.

I was a blur of emotions—joy, worry, happiness, fear. All the good ones. I put the spirit box in the closet before sadly surveying my untidy clothing. If Joey saw this, he'd have a cow. Or a stroke, depending on what mood he was in. He regularly used both euphemisms.

After tending to myself and pondering starting my laundry, I crawled into bed and listened to the rain. I reminisced about this evening's events and quickly fell asleep, which wasn't normal for me. Sleep rarely came easily.

The blaring alarm clock woke me up. After some quick math, I figured I'd only had about four hours of sleep.

Coffee...I needed coffee.

After the second cup, I walked to my computer to check my email. I was surprised to see an email from Kevin, complete with attachment. The subject line read JOEY LACOSTE.

I swallowed as I put my cup down on the desk and clicked on the email.

Naturally, my internet slowed down momentarily, and it took forever for the picture to load. When it did, it took my breath away.

Joey! It was my friend!

I stared at the photograph. Joey Lacoste had been born on April 6, 1977 in Baton Rouge, Louisiana. He had been pursuing a degree in art but also minored in acting. His parents Rhett and Marie Lacoste only had one child, and both were deceased. He had no major medical problems, no tattoos, and no criminal history.

There were other tidbits, but it was so much to take in. I had to know what happened to him and how he died.

My friend, Joey Lacoste. *I miss you, Joey.*

He was killed at the Ridaught Plantation on the same desolate road as Aaron, only a few weeks before him.

Why was this bit of property so attractive to murderers? Two young men murdered on the road behind the house with just weeks between them. Aaron was looking for Joey. He must have known Joey had been here, but how and why?

I wanted to cry, but I was in shock. I sent Kevin an email to thank him for the information and clicked through to the last page of the report. I wondered how much trouble he would get in for sharing this with me. I'd have to see that nobody knew about it.

Nobody but Chloe.

I scanned the page and easily found the death certificate. Under Manner of Death, the coroner had Joey's death marked Undetermined. What did that mean? Not a murder? Further notifications classified Joey's death as a drug toxicity death, probable heroin.

Heroin?

I clicked the printer icon and stared for another ten minutes at my late friend's photo. This made no sense.

Joey had died of a drug overdose? That couldn't be true.

"Hey, I'm going for a cinnamon roll run. You want one?" Chloe popped her head into the office, but her smile vanished immediately.

"What is it? Is that Joey?"

There was no sense in denying the truth. Joey stared back at us from the grainy photograph. His youthful face gleamed slightly. Like all young people, he probably believed he would live forever. It was weird studying him like this without him poking out his tongue or asking, "What? Do I have spinach in my teeth? A flag in my nose?" He had wide hazel eyes I knew occasionally appeared green. They were narrow but easily conveyed his emotions. He had a full bottom lip, the same one he poked out when things did not go his way. His long bangs hung off to the side, and he held his head a jaunty angle.

"Tamara? That's him, isn't it? I need you to say it."

"It's him, Chloe." I handed her the freshly printed papers. She might as well know the whole sad truth. Observing her as she scanned the documents, her defiance showed she'd come to the same conclusion as me. She didn't believe for one minute Joey had overdosed. Why would they classify the nature of his death as undetermined if there wasn't some kind of evidence that disproved an accidental overdose?

She squinted at the paper as she began reading the death certificate aloud. "Aaron came here looking for him, and Aaron was murdered. What was his method of death again?" Chloe asked as she put the papers on my desk.

"Strangulation. On the road back there, but he was found in his car. Joey was found near that spot too. Just a few yards away."

"How did Joey get here? Did he walk? Did he drive? If there was no vehicle, someone dropped him off and left him. Someone murdered Joey, Tamara. Oh, God! This is so horrible! I can't believe what a lousy friend I've been to him. Such a lousy friend, calling him the Ghost and refusing to let him in my room. I never knew he was a murder victim."

Chloe sat in the chair beside me. She was plum shaking and almost hyperventilating. "Whoa, whoa, whoa, Chloe. It's an undetermined death. We don't know for sure that he was murdered. I'm with you, I believe they are related, but we don't know for sure. I would have never guessed Mrs. Loper hung herself from our chandelier or that she was an evil twin. Let's make a list of questions, and I'll email them to Kevin to get his input. While he's checking those out, we need to go back to the road. It has to be us. Me and you."

She slapped her knees in frustration. "You're right. We have to help Aaron and Joey. We have to do it for them. This isn't right. What happened to them is not right at all." I squeezed her hand in silent agreement.

No, it wasn't right, but the only thing we could do for either of them was help them pass over.

And say goodbye forever.

16

CHLOE

Tamara and I trudged through the overgrown yard and stood by the side of the road where Joey died. As I had done quite a few times in recent days, I reached out to him with my mind, but he was quiet. Wherever Joey was and whatever he was doing, he was unable to communicate with me. Whether on purpose or not, it still hurt, and I felt a tremendous amount of guilt. No matter what nice things Tamara said to me, no matter how much Lynn tried to encourage me, the truth was, I had been the one to put Joey in harm's way.

As it turned out, I wasn't the first.

Tamara insisted on bringing her spirit box, but I was pretty sure we were not going to need much in the way of equipment. My emotions were running wild, which always made me an open channel. The chances were good at least one dead person around here was going to head my way, so I had it in my mind I needed to work quickly. As we trudged through the grass, I began visualizing light around me. Light made it easier for me to be found. I told myself to breathe normally and remembered nothing could harm me as long as I stayed in the light.

I decided to put that light around Tamara too. Joey I trusted, and even though I didn't know Aaron, I had no reason to suspect he was anything but good. But if there was a killer, if there was someone killing young men even back in the '90s, he could still be here. He could be dead. Evil dead often return to the places where they wreaked the most havoc.

Two young men dead? I'd say that was pretty evil.

As we passed a clump of wildflowers, I paused to pluck them. It was only right that we bring some kind of tribute to the two forgotten souls. I guessed this was kind of a memorial.

A tribute to Joey and Aaron.

Before we even cleared the ditch, I knew he was there. I could feel Aaron's heartbreaking vibration and his over-whelming sadness. He was waiting for us as if he'd known we were coming. He'd known one day he would have to face this moment.

You don't have to be afraid, Aaron. We are here to help you. We are Joey's friends, and we want to be yours too.

To my surprise, the young dead man fled from me. He only went as far as the other side of the road, but it was enough of a distance to let me know he wasn't prepared for this transition. And he wasn't communicating with me, not yet.

"He's not ready to move on, Tamara. I'm kind of glad you brought that because he's not talking either. I guess we should start here." I paced a few steps and quickly picked up on the spot where one or both of the young men had died.

This death had left a strange signature. I glanced over my shoulder and was relieved to see there was no sign of the Reaper, but he would be coming soon. He'd been hanging around waiting for Mrs. Loper, but he hadn't been able to collect her.

She had passed through the door without any intervention from him. The Reaper would miss this one too. I hoped he wouldn't hold a grudge.

Okay, Chloe. Get your mind under control. Don't forget you aren't the only one listening.

"Why don't you get started? He might be more apt to talk to you, Tamara."

She put the box on the ground and turned on the power. I'd seen quite a bit of this machine recently. She liked it a lot, and one good thing about it was it recorded your session. Chances were if we got anything from Aaron, anything valuable at all, having a recording would make it more impressive for Deputy Patrick. I gave him props for keeping an open mind.

"Aaron, my name is Tamara. I was here before, but I'm here today with Chloe. We know about Joey. We know he was your friend." Random static issued from the black box. It was an annoying sound, like listening to someone changing the radio station about five times a second. It was extremely irritating, but I immediately detected a voice.

Joey...I'm sorry...

Tamara's eyes widened, but she continued her attempts

at communicating with the murdered young man. "Aaron? Do you know where Joey is? Do you know what happened to him?" The spirit box began flipping through the stations even faster. I wasn't sure how this equipment worked, but I was under the impression it couldn't fluctuate like that. Maybe I was wrong. It was hard to tell since the world was spinning and I felt woozy.

Very woozy.

I staggered on my feet, but Tamara was right there. "I'm good. I'm feeling him. Aaron...were you getting high out here? Is that what you are doing behind the house?"

The entire experience was freaking me out. I'd never done hard drugs, even though a lot of kids at our school did, but I guzzled a wine cooler once, and this was a similar feeling, only much more intense.

Yes.

Without much warning, I was sitting in a car with Aaron and Joey. They were in the front seat, music was blaring, and there was a purple sky. I couldn't feel or hear Joey's mind, but I was connected with Aaron. He wasn't really a bad guy. He wanted me to know that right off the bat before he went any further. His eyes caught mine in the rearview mirror. Joey didn't seem to notice me. He was singing along to the song and drinking his beer.

Totally oblivious to what was about to happen.

I can feel you are not a bad guy. What happened, Aaron?

Aaron's eyes left mine, and he smiled at the young man beside him. He couldn't believe Joey had agreed to come out here. They kissed again. They had been kissing all night, but not much else had happened. Aaron got the vibe that Joey was inexperienced, and in many ways was an innocent. That was one of the reasons why Aaron was so attracted to him. He could see himself in Joey. He had never imagined himself in a long-term relationship with a guy. Nobody knew about him and his preferences, but Joey was dreamy, and he had a poet's heart. A true poet. Yeah, he could steal my heart if I let him.

Aaron had never met anyone who wrote poetry until he met Joey. They went to the same college, but Aaron was not enrolled in any of the arts courses. He was a numbers guy from top to bottom, or at least he used to be before this all started.

I'm not a bad guy. I swear. I didn't know.

What happened? Show me?

Aaron's sad eyes met mine briefly in the rearview mirror again, and I watched as he removed a small leopard print case from his glove box. He observed Joey's body tensing as he produced the surprise, further proof his partner was very inexperienced. He might even be a virgin. That thought amused Aaron and aroused him. Up until this moment, he didn't believe there was still such a thing as virginity or innocence. Not in his world.

Aaron's community was hardcore partiers, a very active group of friends who didn't observe limits. He'd been pressured to bring Joey into their inner circle, which made this even more heartbreaking.

For the first time ever, he wanted to keep someone for himself. Someone who would laugh at his jokes. Someone who might enjoy his cooking and his humor. Aaron chewed the inside of his lip as he pondered all this. Ace's voice rang in my mind. He wanted more inroads here at the college, essentially more addicts. People who wanted his powder. Pretty ones like Joey.

"You've got one job, Aaron. All you were asked to do was get familiar with the kid. That's all. Don't screw this up. You'll need more, you know you will."

As if it were a final warning, a bright star blasted through the sky. It passed right beyond the house, which was ridiculous because stars were much farther away. No, that star had flamed out far away from this place.

Kind of like me.

My star was flaming out. I was losing everything, even my edge. My scholarship was shot, and without it, there was no way I was getting in next semester. I chewed my bottom lip, and suddenly Joey was there. He kissed me tenderly, and I kissed him back.

"Try it with me? Just a little?"

Aaron showed him the case with the two needles and the powdery substance.

"Stop it! Tamara, oh, my God!" I reached for her hand. Even though I couldn't see her, I needed to know she was there. I had to be able to come back from this horrible moment.

"I'm here. I'm right here. What's going on? Talk to me, Chloe."

"It's okay. I'm okay. I have to see this." I stared into the rearview mirror. I witnessed Joey's hesitation.

Joey flashed his glamorous smile and shook his head. Although Aaron was moved by his refusal, he was the kind of guy who preferred getting his way. "Do we really need that?"

Aaron's stubbornness had been a problem in past relationships, but he wasn't thinking about self-improvement. He was thinking about how much he wanted to be with Joey, and he wanted to share this experience with his new lover. At least, he hoped they would be lovers. They weren't there yet. He hadn't sealed the deal yet, but he was close.

"You saw that star? That's how good this is. We could be together, and I'm sure it'll be great, but if we want that shooting star experience, this is how we do it."

I held my breath as I watched Joey pull back from Aaron. He tilted his head. It was a typical Joey move when he heard something he didn't like, or he didn't quite believe what you were saying.

"How many times have you done this? I mean, with someone else?"

Aaron's smile was disarming. He was much like Joey in that his easy nature made you want to trust him. I knew the truth because I saw things through Aaron's eyes.

I'm not a bad guy.

I refrained from responding to his intrusive thought, but it was really hard for me to accept that statement as truth, and getting harder by the minute.

"Come on. What kind of question is that? I'm not hooking up with people out here on a regular basis if that's what you're thinking. It's cool. I thought maybe you'd want to try it, but it's cool."

Aaron snapped the case shut and tossed it on the dashboard. His words said one thing, but his behavior said something altogether different. He turned his face away from Joey, propped his elbow against the door, and cradled his chin thoughtfully. It was a pose that had come in handy for him. People always thought he was a deep thinker, but he wasn't thinking all that deeply.

Not beyond the next fix. The next hook-up.

With all my mind, I wanted to scream, "You *are* a bad guy!" For Joey's sake, I kept my mouth shut and watched it unfold before me.

"I'll try it, but I don't know how to do any of this. I guess you know I'm kind of a rookie." From the mirror, I could see Joey's eyes were good and bloodshot. They had probably kicked back more than one beer.

I sobbed in the backseat, but nobody paid me any attention, and I couldn't move. Tamara was clutching my hand, but I couldn't hear what she was saying. I was determined to see it through. I couldn't step away from the vision now.

It was a weird sensation, being in the past and the present at the same time. I didn't want to see Joey die, but I knew it was coming. This was not the narrative I'd created in my mind. There was no ominous bad guy out there.

No one but you, Aaron. You *are* a bad guy!

There it was, in black and white—my honest thought about this whole thing. This whole sordid affair. Just as I was ready to step away, to move back into the present and leave the past behind, I heard Aaron's voice.

I have to show you. Please, let me show you.

I didn't verbally consent, but something inside me invited this disclosure. Suddenly, the film I was watching went into fast speed. I saw it all. Aaron and Joey together in the car and using the kit, only something went wrong.

Aaron panicked and cried, but in the end, he did the wrong thing. In his intoxication, he rolled Joey out of the car and down the ditch. He wasn't sure if Joey was dead.

He thought maybe he felt a pulse, but then it was gone, and he was so high he forgot Joey was there.

For how long? He couldn't remember that either. He woke up in the car, and it was deep into the night. There wasn't a hint of light behind the old Ridaught Plantation. And there was no evidence Joey had ever been there, except his beer bottle in the car. He tossed it into the ditch with Joey and didn't look back.

He cried all the way home and for several days after that, but he never told anyone. The weird thing was his friends, the guys interested in Joey? They didn't even mention him.

It was as if Joey had only been a blip on their radar. He'd been like a star that pulsated once and disappeared into the blackness.

Just when Aaron began to convince himself Joey was alive and that he wasn't dead, he saw his face in the newspaper.

Young Man Found Dead Behind Abandoned Mansion.

There was the evidence of his soul-crushing sin. For the next few weeks, he pondered what to do.

Who should he talk to? The cops? His dad was a cop. No. He and the old man never saw eye to eye on much of anything. If he told his father the truth about what happened, his old man certainly wouldn't approve of any of it. He damn sure wouldn't approve of the fact Aaron had left his friend to die in a ditch by himself.

Going to the cops was a horrible idea, and the thought of coming down from his beloved heroin in jail made him even sicker. He couldn't do it. There was only one thing he could do.

There had only been one solution to begin with. All this partying, it had just been a delay tactic for the inevitable. He knew what he had to do. This was a kind of penance. As he pulled the car behind the house, his eyes fell on the yellow police tape.

Solid evidence of his unforgivable sin.

Joey didn't deserve what happened to him. He didn't deserve to be tossed out of the car like rubbish. He didn't deserve to be forgotten and unloved.

I couldn't make it right, but I could do this.

I could punish his killer.

I spent days researching how to do it. There were a lot of ways one could commit suicide. Drugs seem to be the top of the list, but it would take a lot to kill me. I'd been getting high for so long, I didn't have that kind of money or time. And I wanted it to end.

Joey had been the one.

I could've loved him forever, but as usual, I could love no one as much as I loved myself. That was my curse. I should never have forced him and coerced him into getting high. I stole his future and mine. I could not live with that.

I put the car in park and flipped the radio on. As if the universe approved of my plan, that song played, the one from that night when this suffocating nightmare began.

I had a plan.

"Please, just tell me." Tears were streaming down my face, and Tamara was shaking my hands and arms. Her screams sounded as if they were coming from deep underwater. I was firmly immersed in the past. With every passing second, I lost confidence that I would be able to come back.

"Aaron, show me, and I promise I'll help you. I will help you step into the light. What did you do?"

The video sped up again. Aaron tied the scarf around the back of the seat and his neck. He tied it so tight it was a struggle to put the needle in his arm, but he managed to do it. Once the poison was in his veins, he eventually sagged, and the silk scarf tightened until he stopped breathing. It did not take long to die.

He hung around the vehicle for a little while and watched his body. It wasn't his father who showed up first, thankfully. The cop recognized him. His last name was Richards. He removed the scarf and pulled the needle out of Aaron's arm. That's when his father showed up. He didn't even cry. He threw his hat across the field and got sick, but he didn't cry. Not a tear. He didn't cry at Aaron's funeral, either. It was as if he'd never mattered.

"Look at me, Aaron. I'm crying. I'm crying for you and Joey. I saw it all. Now it's time to go."

But Joey. If I could see him...

I winced at the idea. There was no way in hell I was going to make that happen, even if Joey had been available and willing. This was the worst-case scenario. Aaron knew that, and he accepted it.

"That has to be up to him, not me. I can help you find peace. You see that light over there?" I visualized the light just a few feet away from Aaron. It was easy to do, maybe because I'd been in the spirit realm so long. I was feeling a strange sense of urgency.

Yes, too long. Go back, Chloe!

Mom? Okay, Mom!

"See the light? There is a door right inside it, Aaron. I know you can see it. That's where the light is coming from, Aaron. Somebody you love, someone you really love is on the other side of that door. It is opening, and you are going to see that person. Think of someone. The person you want to see the most." I was weeping as I coached him toward the light.

Joey. I want to see Joey.

"I can't make that happen. Maybe that's your punishment, Aaron. Maybe that's how you pay your penance. Someday you might see him, but not here. You have to go."

He sighed, and I knew I'd won him over. He walked toward the door but paused before reaching for it. I held my breath as I watched and waited for him to make his final move. I couldn't force him. I would never do that. This had to be his decision, but it would be best for him to leave. Best for Joey too.

"What about your mother? Is she there? Can you see her?" It was a guess and apparently a lucky one, because his expression changed. There was no more hesitation. No more fear or guilt. He smiled, and it was a peaceful sight. I cried hard for Aaron, even though he'd caused the death of my friend. I didn't understand how the light could accept people like Mrs. Loper and Aaron, but I was glad it did. I was glad I didn't have to be their judge.

Tell him I'm sorry.

I made him no promise, only nodded, and then he was gone. Aaron was gone, and I would never see him again.

I was glad for that.

"Chloe? Can you hear me?" To my surprise, I was

looking up at Tamara. How had I gotten on the ground? Where had the cop come from?

"Hey. Yeah, I can hear you. Help me up."

Kevin squatted beside me and warned me to take my time getting up. "Slow and easy. Move slow and easy. How are you feeling now? Any pain?"

With fierceness, I hugged Tamara. She hugged me back, and together we cried. Tamara didn't know why she was crying, and I loved that about her.

"I'm okay, Aunt Tamara. I'm really okay. Take me home, please. I want to go home."

"Sure, let's go. Let's ride with Kevin. You can leave those flowers for Joey and Aaron. We will bring more tomorrow." She rubbed my back and sat with me in the back of the vehicle. I laid my head on her shoulder, and when we got in the house, I told them both everything.

Tamara cried, hearing how Joey had died. Kevin immediately began making phone calls. At least the truth would come out, and Joey would have some closure. Maybe Aaron too.

When the time came and Joey was ready to talk about it, I would be there for him. I'd never call him the Ghost again. He deserved more from the people he loved. He deserved more than what he got from Aaron, a guy he trusted.

That night before I went to bed, I did something I hadn't done in a long time. I said a prayer. It was hokey and not very religious, but I did it nonetheless. I prayed for Mom, Aaron, and Joey. Especially Joey. I prayed everyone would be covered in light.

When I woke up the following morning, all of the heaviness of the prior evening's activities had faded. I felt lighter and better.

More hopeful.

An idea popped into my head. I had a project I wanted to tackle. I couldn't do it by myself. I would need Tamara's help, but I was going to make it happen.

This would be fun!

EPILOGUE—TAMARA

After listening to the phone ding multiple times as I had my hands in dishwater, I decided to check out my notifications. There wasn't much in the way of email, but my Periscope account had exploded with new views and subscribers. People were commenting left and right. I could hardly believe it. Even more surprisingly, Kevin was recommending my channel to his friends. I would never have guessed he would be so open to the paranormal.

Joey had been right; the camera did add at least ten pounds, and the wide lens was not my friend. I would have never done anything like pitch a show called *Stripper Supernatural,* but I was a good investigator and an intuitive person. Not a true medium like Chloe, but I had some skills. If only I trusted my intuition.

I'd have to if I was going to help Chloe get established here and I was going to have a life beyond and after the Dead House.

Damn it, Joey. I miss you. Why did you have to leave?

Before I could put the phone back on the charger, I received a text from Kevin. Hunky, bigger than life, handcuff-slinging Kevin. He wanted to stop by after his shift, and of course I said yes. He wouldn't wrap up until ten, but I was cool with that. I'd always been a night owl, even before working in nightclubs and the like.

I wondered how much I should tell him about my past, and whether I should tell him anything. No, not yet. Why ruin a good thing? If he ran for sheriff, then yes, of course, I would. It might matter who he was dating, but then again, it might not. It wasn't like we're getting married or anything. It wasn't like that at all. We were just two grownups having fun.

There you go, Tamara Garvey. Overthinking everything. Absolutely everything.

I sent him back a winking girl emoji and a mildly flirty text. I put the phone back and left the kitchen after I locked the back door and turned out the overhead light. Except for the light over the sink; I always left that light on.

Just in case Joey wanted to find his way home.

I'd printed the first draft of my outline earlier, and it was waiting for me in the living room, along with a few snacks and a bottle of water. I couldn't bring myself to make popcorn, not without Joey. I'd take a shower soon, but for now, I wanted to binge-watch the *Dead Files* and proof my notes.

There was always something to add or subtract. Writing challenged me, and I liked a good challenge. It was easy to skip over important details the first go-around, and it was tempting to waste words on describing dress fabrics or sounds and expressions. My dialogue sometimes came off as repetitive, but I'd get better at this whole writing thing. I was sure of it. I just needed practice and patience. I was always short on that.

Chloe wasn't home tonight. She was working her new job at the ice cream shop, and she was driving my car. Chloe was a more careful driver than me, but I wouldn't rest until she was home.

Psychic Amy was deep into her first investigation when I finished my first proofread. It needed more work, but at least I knew how the story ended for Aaron. So heartbreaking.

We were still working on breaking the ancestral curse. Suddenly, the couch sagged a little beside me. Just like it always did when Joey plopped down on it.

Nobody ever sat there, not even Chloe and strangely enough, not Kevin. Chloe had her own chair, and she didn't hang out in the living room much anymore. She preferred her bedroom for studying or the kitchen for hanging out with me when she wasn't plundering the attic.

I held my breath as I put the manuscript down on the coffee table. Was I imagining this just because I wanted to see him? "Joey? Is that you?"

"Who else would it be? I'm irreplaceable. No matter what you do in the car."

"Joey!" I started to scold him for being so nosy, but I was so glad he was here, I didn't allow myself to get too worked up. "I'm so glad you're here. Where have you been? Was it hard to get back?"

As elusive as always, he asked, "Where else would I be? Is this another rerun? Oh, poor Ames. She looks so haggard. I hope she learns to rest between investigations.

They pack far too many episodes into one season." Joey's outline appeared on the couch beside me. He was as he always was, maybe a little faded. He wore his slouchy blue jeans and an old t-shirt. His hair, a little long, was golden-blonde. His eyes were always hurt, which made you love him even more.

Instinctively, I reached beside me on the couch as if I could actually hold his hand. I could not. Not today. He wasn't solid at all. He was weak, far too weak to manifest. He really needed some energy. I started getting cold. I shoved the blanket up around my legs and put my hands in my lap. I couldn't help but smile at him as a tear or two slid down my cheeks.

"Come on, I wasn't gone that long."

"I thought you left after Aaron crossed over, and I wouldn't have blamed you if you did. I really wouldn't have blamed you. I know, I mean, I think I know how you felt about him. I am so sorry about what happened to you and to him. I don't even know what to say."

Joey watched the television for a few seconds, but he put his hand over mine. "I can't leave you, Tamara. You're a train wreck."

I buried my face in my hands at the heartbreak of it all. "I missed you, Joey. Chloe is going to be so happy to hear you're home. She felt so bad for what she did that she put you at risk, but you protected her. Thank you, Joey! I can't believe you did that. Are you crazy?" I went from crying to yelling at him. Apparently, this was one episode he hadn't seen yet. "Have I told you I missed you?"

"Of course, you missed me. I'm fabulous. I took a look at your new outline. Pardon me for not reading your manuscript." He waved his hand at the stack of paper on the coffee table. I would never have expected him to read the story of his own death. I had dedicated it to him, though.

"The outline isn't bad, but I'm not sure you've got the chandelier scene right. She did have help getting up that ladder. That servant of hers, Anita, she was in on it. She wanted Lavinia to die. Anita wasn't a bad woman, but she was afraid of Mrs. Loper, and I think she thought she was helping the girls. When Lavinia asked her about doing it, she didn't hesitate. But it was Mrs. Loper who initiated the curse. The one that fell on Annabel and, of course, now our Chloe. I don't even think she meant to do it."

I sipped my water and put it back on the table beside me. "Wow, I didn't see that plot twist coming. That's how Lavinia had all those impact injuries. She'd fallen from the chandelier instead of just hanging. So, are you saying her neck was broken, but she survived the fall? Damn! She would have had multiple injuries. That drop should have killed her. No wonder the chandelier had been going crazy." I paused for a moment. "How did she get up the stairs afterward then?"

"Mr. Loper found her and carried her up there. I think he thought she was dead, and his daughter was dead too, but the little girl died naturally from a virus or the flu. That's not quite clear to me. He put them together out of kindness. Then Mrs. Loper started moving and moaning. He was trying to reset her bones. As damaged as she was, it would be easy for a sick person to misconstrue his help for hurt."

I thought about his statement and then further questioned him. "How do you know all this?"

"When you're dead, you can do a lot of things, like go back in time. I just have no future."

That solemn statement shut down the conversation for a few minutes.

It was tragic to imagine yet another lost soul roamed the Dead House, but at least Chloe could help them cross over. First Annie Hensley, then Mrs. Loper, and now Aaron. But not Joey. Why did I feel bad about that? I didn't want him to stay here because of me. Maybe he wasn't. I would just have to enjoy the time I had with him.

"Kevin's coming over later, Joey. You'll have to get lost when he's here. And no peeping, not even once!" I joked with him as he tilted his head and put his hand over his lips.

"Your secrets are safe with me, Tamara Garvey. All of them. Has he seen the fuzzy bra yet or the leather teddy? I'm not sure Deputy Kevin is ready for you, wild child."

I thought about smacking him with a pillow, but that wouldn't do any good. He laughed and tossed his hair back before hitting the remote button.

"You're such a liar, Joey. You know you spy on me."

"That's rude. I would never do that. Now Kevin, I might spy on him." Suddenly Joey flickered like someone unplugged him temporarily.

"What's going on? Are you sick, Joey?" Can dead people be sick?

"Chloe's mother, Tina Louise, drained me. It's their curse. It took a lot to make a connection with her. I'll recover, sweet cheeks." It was weird having a conversation with a disembodied voice, even a voice I knew so well. I wasn't afraid, but it gave me the chill bumps.

"I'm working on it. I think I may have someone who can help us break the curse. Her name is Angela Webster. She's supposed to get back to me soon. Do you think Chloe is in danger?"

Joey's sad voice worried me. "I don't know, honestly. I sure can't take Chloe back to ask. That crazy Annabel wants to kill her. She's probably around, and she's really pissed but about what I don't know. She doesn't want anyone here, especially Chloe."

Joey flickered back into view, and this time he was standing beside me with a beer in his hand. Not a real beer, of course. I didn't drink that brand. At least it wasn't that raggedy cat again.

"By the way, Tina Louise is beautiful, like a supermodel, and way taller than you, shorty."

"Hey!" I said at his assertion I was too short. He wasn't wrong of course, but I could rock a pair of four-inch heels as well as anyone. I had a stunning high heel collection, even though I rarely wore them anymore.

"You can feel something fierce within her. That family, the Ridaught women—they have a strength about them, Chloe has it too. It separates them from others. She had a very strong will in her day, I imagine. But she's gone now, Tamara. Tina Louise is gone. She's going to wait on the other side for Chloe. It's safer for her. Oh, I almost forgot, Tina Louise says thank you for the birthday cards."

"She read them?" I clutched the blanket to my chest. "Really?"

"Yes, and she's really upset with you." Joey grew a little more luminous now.

"Me? Why?" I was completely stymied. "What did I do?"

He put his hand on his sexy hip. "You let that lawyer pull a fast one on you. You didn't get it all. She left Chloe a second trust. A large trust. He's stealing from Chloe. She says fix it or she will!" He rubbed his forehead as if he were getting a headache. I could barely breathe. That meant all this time I'd been busting my ass trying to make a new life for Chloe, hustling here and there to make ends meet. I mean, the advance royalty check from the publishing company was nice, but it wouldn't last forever.

"I'll talk to Kevin about finding a good attorney. I'm sure he can help me."

"Get a vicious one and force him to honor the agreement."

"I will, I swear! Tell her not to worry." I glanced at my watch. "Oh, shoot! Kevin is going to be here soon. Joey, I want to show you something. It's a surprise. Can you keep your eyes closed and follow my voice?"

He squealed and clapped his hands as his beer disappeared. "I think so. Wait. Like, a real surprise? This isn't some lame trick, is it?"

"Joey, it's me. Of course not. I love you, my friend. To be fair, this surprise was Chloe's idea to start with. I don't want to take all the credit for it. Come up the stairs with me. I want to show you something. I was praying we could give this to you together, but I can't wait!" He squealed like a kid and jumped up and down again. "Close your eyes!"

"Okay! Take my hand. A surprise, and it's not even my birthday!"

"But you're home. That's all that matters. Come on, up the steps." I smiled at Joey's closed eyes. I was feeling kind of sick and definitely low energy, which meant Joey was getting stronger because of me. I'd have to say goodbye to him soon to stop myself from getting even sicker. He'd understand; he always did. He'd probably go next door and drain Linda Blabbermouth if they hadn't moved out yet.

I opened the door to the newly remodeled guest room. I held Joey's hand and left him standing in the center of the room with his eyes closed. I walked over to the radio and turned it on. I had a tape cued up and ready to go. Simple Minds began playing Joey's favorite song, *Don't You Forget About Me*. He didn't open his eyes, but now it was his turn to cry. I flicked on the black light and the lava lamp. "Open those eyes, handsome!"

"What?" he said as he spun about the room to take it all in.

"I know you're a nineties guy. I went with gray for the walls, because you know, the whole grunge look and believe it or not, gray is still in style. The bed is not a king, but it is a queen, which I thought was suitable. You've got ample storage in here, and you can do anything you like with the room. If you want to change the paint color, add twinkle lights, whatever you want, we can make it happen. This is your room, Joey. It's only a few doors down from Chloe, but she's okay with it. But remember, don't go into Chloe's room unless invited. Even I have to follow that rule."

Joey sat on the bed and stared at the posters on the wall. Pearl Jam, Nirvana, and R.E.M. stared down at Joey and he quickly got up to examine each of them. His legs weren't manifested, but he was excitedly talking about concerts and singers and who was dead and who was alive.

"You did this for me? Really? Chloe probably hates it, though."

"No, this was her idea. She wanted you to have a place to come back to. No more hiding in dryers, and definitely no more putting your head in the oven. Don't lose hope, Joey. As long as you want to be here, it's yours."

"I don't know what to say," he said as he touched the vintage Pearl Jam poster. "This is so thoughtful. You know I'm not this sentimental. I may change a few things, but I love it! Thank you, Tamara Garvey! This is the nicest thing anyone has ever done for me. I really do love it!"

"Good. Well, do you mind getting lost for a while? My date is coming over. And remember you promised no peeking at any bare asses." He groaned but immediately began playing with the lights. He was causing them to flicker off and on just by waving his fingers.

"I love it. I can't believe y'all did this for me. I can't say thank you enough. Close the door behind you, Tamara, and pay no mind if I play the music a bit loud. My own room! It's been a long time since I've had my own room. What time does Chloe get home?"

I smiled at him as I went to the door. "She'll be home about ten o'clock. Should I text her that you're here? She's going to be so happy to see you. Chloe has been over-whelmed with guilt."

"No, please don't. I want to surprise her." He smiled, and his beautiful smile lit up the room. He was happy and ultra-luminous. I couldn't say no. I glanced at my watch again. I better get downstairs. I wouldn't have time for a shower, but it didn't matter. "Bye, Joey. Promise me you won't go anywhere? You'll stay here with us, won't you?"

"It's not like I have anything else to do. I'm always dead. That's not going to change."

"You don't have to keep bringing that up. I didn't mean it that way. I better go. I think that's Kevin's car pulling in the driveway. Chloe will be here soon. See you later, Joey. Right?"

"Right," he smiled back, and to my surprise, Joey kissed me right on the lips, but it wasn't all romantic and mushy. It was more like a friendly kiss. I mean obviously, I wasn't interested in him nor he me, despite our talk about 2.5 kids and the white picket fence. To my further surprise, his lips weren't cold.

"Why did you do that?" I could hardly move. I wasn't sure how to proceed at all.

"I don't know. Go have fun, Tamara. Leave me your phone, though, because I want to watch your Periscope."

"You aren't getting my phone. Besides, you have a television of your own. Watch your shows. I'll see you later. Good night, Joey."

He grinned as he spun in the center of the room. "Good night, Tamara. I'll wait up for you."

I smiled at that. "What if he spends the night?"

"I'll still wait up for you."

I smiled, feeling happy and hopeful. "Good night, Joey. I'll see you in the morning."

With that, I closed the door. I practically skipped down the steps. I was so happy.

I had my family back together again. My family!

The doorbell rang, and I smiled as I hurried down the

stairs. I was happy to see the new chandelier was behaving. There were no bloody bodies lying around. The music thumped and pumped from the second floor, old nineties tunes. I knew Joey would love the song by U2. How sad was it that I still made mixtapes?

I mean come on, Tamara, it's 2020.

Kevin walked in with a bunch of flowers, a bottle of wine, and a face full of razor cuts. Apparently, his razor had been a dull one, but it was sweet of him to try to look nice for me. Here I was without my shower.

"Chloe home? I didn't see your car in the driveway," he asked. I kissed him passionately. Oh, Joey. Forgive me. Your kiss was sweet, the kiss of a friend, but I need Kevin. He is alive and real, and I think...yes, I think we might have something together.

"Joey's back. You'll see him later, I'm sure of it. For now, I have something else planned. Chloe is coming home soon, and I'm dying for a shower. What do you think?"

"I just took a shower. Oh, you want me to...hell yeah, I'd like to take a shower. Lead the way!" Kevin kissed me again with his lopsided smile and warm hands on my skin. We chunked the wine and flowers on the entryway table. I had other things to think about.

We heard footsteps upstairs. Joey was singing in his room. Having the time of his life, my Joey, the eternal twenty-year-old. As he said, he was always dead.

For me, I would grab my happiness with both hands. I closed the door to my bedroom and even went to the trouble of hanging a tie on the door, in case anyone got any ideas about knocking. I played some music of my own and then led my half-naked, then fully naked sheriff's deputy into the shower for a half-hour of playtime. It was worth every minute of it.

We left the shower squeaky clean but still hungry for one another. At least I was still hungry for Kevin. I had a feeling I would be for a really long time too. Later, as we lay in bed and talked quietly about our day. I heard Chloe's happy scream. She and Joey frolicked around, and he was clearly happy about his room.

"Sounds like she found him," I whispered, but Kevin was softly snoring. They played music for another hour and then it all went quiet. The whole house was bathed in silence.

Kevin had fallen asleep rather quickly, and to my relief, he slept hard. I had always been a light sleeper. It wasn't a stretch to say I preferred being awake to being asleep.

I slid out of the sheets and put on my leggings and a baggy t-shirt. I quietly walked out of the room and closed the door behind me.

Joey was waiting up for me. It was his first night back since he'd been gone. But gone to where? I'd like to know but probably never would.

Sure enough, Joey was sitting on the couch, glowing brightly and watching some paranormal show. One he didn't like too much. *Spirit Adventures*, I think it was called.

"Well, how was it?" He smirked and tilted his head slightly in my direction.

"I don't kiss and tell," I answered.

"Fair enough. Change of subject." I watched him carefully in hopes of gauging his reaction.

"Tell me about your love life. I bet it was much more exciting than mine. Until recently."

He shook his long bangs, and they covered his eyes. "I don't kiss and tell either."

I sighed with happiness. "I'm glad you're home, Joey. Don't leave again."

"I don't plan on it, Priscilla. What's up with that bouffant? Please don't bring it back. That hairstyle should never have happened. Oh, never mind. I guess you were on bottom tonight?" I slung a throw pillow in his direction, and it landed soundly on his chest. That was a good sign. If he was getting back to being strong enough to interact with his surroundings, he was on his way to recovery. "Now go back to bed. I don't want you snoring in here. I can watch this by myself. I know you aren't that keen on *Spirit Adventures.*"

I smiled at him. "Really? You would be okay watching this by yourself? You are going to freak yourself out, you know."

"Good night, Tamara. Give my love to Kevin."

I laughed at that idea. "Um, I'd rather not. But good night, Joey. Stay out of trouble."

"I'm dead, what can I possibly do?" That's when I noticed my purse on the couch. How did it get in here?

I laughed at his pretend innocence. I picked up my purse and carried it back to my bedroom with me.

Just in case Joey decided to get overly excited about some infomercial in the middle of the night. Like the one selling heated pillows or 360 sunglasses, the special kind that allowed you to see behind you. Or a hundred other things he couldn't use.

But we were home and all together.

My strange and wonderfully weird family.

At last.

The End

Continue following Tamara, Chloe and Joey's adventures in Dead House with the next book, *Dead At Midnight*, coming soon to Amazon and Kindle Unlimited.

AUTHOR'S NOTE

Hey there! Thank you for reading *Always Dead*, Book Two in the *Welcome to Dead House* series. It was a fun project to work on. I love spending time with Tamara, Joey, Chloe, and all the ghosts of the Ridaught Plantation. I have a feeling we will be seeing more of them in the near future. I love the Dead House!

I have a real soft spot for Tamara Garvey. She's fun, wild, and yet a real character to me. To be honest, I never thought I'd write a character that was so much like me in so many ways. She's Southern and sassy, kind of finding her way a little later in life. That's so me. There are other similarities too. Let me explain a little.

Better still, let me make a confession to you: I worked in burlesque for a full ten years in the 1990s, and I loved every minute of it. Just for the record, burlesque was and is a very different thing than being an exotic dancer. Burlesque revolves around storytelling, flirtatious teasing, and a peek at skin every now and then. Stripping isn't like that at all. I feel very fortunate to have learned the art from some amazing artists.

The burlesque clubs and venues I worked at back then were often old buildings with ornate stages and crowded dressing rooms. The old burlesque theaters scattered hither and yon are now most likely put to very different uses. I always say I want to go back and see them, but I really don't. (I would die if I drove back to the East Coast to see the Fuzzy Grape and found only a parking lot.)

Our sets were made for performers, and our props were always dramatic and interesting. Putting together sets, selecting music, arranging special effects, I got quite good at handling my own production details.

Traveling up the Eastern Seaboard from Baltimore to Connecticut to Massachusetts and then later New York was an amazing journey. Times were so different from today, and it was not that long ago. After my ten-year tour, I returned home to live in the South, where I planned to spend the rest of my life.

Alabama had always been home to me, but I had so much fun in New England. Nice people up there, and believe it or not, they have a soft spot for their favorite blonde Southerner. (That's *moi*, y'all!) Although that portion of my life is over, I'm technically too old to be a showgirl at this point, I still crave adventure and exploring interesting places. Trips to Egypt and Greece are on my bucket list. And because of my writing, I won't have to remove a single article of clothing to get there.

But a part of me wonders if those clubs could be haunted.

Haunted by the fans? Haunted by the entertainers who loved those places?

There was a lot of energy released in those places. (Pardon the pun.) Roaring crowds of men, and some women. Thumping music, excited performers. (Hmm...maybe I should go back for a paranormal investigation. Wouldn't that be a hoot?)

Like Tamara and her friend Tina Louise, I had to travel with heavy trunks full of costumes. Long velvet beaded gowns that zipped up the side, over the top hats, ridiculous heels. I also had oversized powder puffs and other such accouterments to tease my fans with. It was a lot of fun, and I'm glad I was able to participate in the art of burlesque entertainment. Many of the entertainers I met were complete professionals, dutiful souls who appreciated the art of true striptease. Like Tamara, I learned a lot about myself during those early days in burlesque. I learned it took courage to put on a show for a group of strangers and to do so confidently.

One night I was Alice in Wonderland and another I was the Jewel of Mumbai with an intricate headpiece and beads everywhere. It was play-acting, and it taught me a lot about being a good character. And later writing them. (At least I hope.)

And I'm happy to say I was a part of that sisterhood. We were actresses all; of the lowest sort if you were to ask more traditional actresses, but we were actresses nonetheless. It was a hoot to learn the traditional dance of the fans from a legend of the stage. I met so many interesting people, especially those costumers and dressmakers. After my character shed her velvet gown and beaded undergarments, I often danced between two fans, artfully avoiding showing too much to the cheering crowd. That was always a challenge.

I'd be lying if I said I didn't miss those days. Who wouldn't miss hearing the roar of the crowd four times a night? How could I not miss dreaming up interesting shows for my fans? I loved burlesque because it allowed me to be creative and to be an artist.

I loved creating personas and characters that people would fall in love with. Literally. I'm so very grateful I took what I learned from those days and was able to apply those skills to writing.

Today, I still enjoy creating personas and characters people fall in love with. I love telling a story and having you stay with me the whole time so you can find out what happens at the end. That is important to me. And although I don't hear the roar of the crowd, I like to imagine I hear you turning the pages. And people are not chanting my stage name at the end of every show, but occasionally I get to sign a book, and even more frequently, I get to spend time with all of you. Usually through social media or one of my events. I treasure those moments, and I love posing for photos.

I get to have fun without balancing fans or tiptoeing around in high heels or hoping the zipper worked on my gown at the right time. That's what I love about writing—about being creative.

I love Tamara because she's a part of me.

I love that she's moved on to explore her new life with writing. I love that she lives in a haunted house and has the chance to help another person learn how to be better.

Chloe needs a mentor, and I can't think of a better person than Tamara Garvey. Tamara will teach her to be kind but also street-smart. Tamara will teach her to be creative but also practical. Tamara will teach her to work hard and believe in herself. That's what she's learning to do too.

About Joey, who doesn't love him? Joey is the guy you almost fall in love with. He's the guy who loves you but not like you need him to. We've all had Joey relationships in our lives, haven't we? I have. Joey is handsome, funny, and incredibly broken. He was broken before his death and is broken still. Leave it to Tamara to want to fix him for his own sake. Joey's life is over, but I look forward to helping him move on one day.

Just not too soon. Not yet.

I don't think he's ready yet, do you? Eventually he needs to cross over and find peace with himself. That's always a challenge when your life has been cut far too short.

But let's see where Joey takes us. He might have ideas of his own. He usually does.

At least he has his own room now. I'm sure he'll find ways to get into mischief before it's all over with.

I look forward to bringing you the next book, and I look forward to seeing you at the Dead House.

Don't forget, if you would like to connect with me, you can find me on Facebook. You can also email me, and you can join my mailing list on my website ML Bullock.com.

Thanks again for reading my stories and for being entertained by them.

All my best,
Monica Leigh Bullock

Want to be notified when my next book releases? <u>Click</u> <u>here</u>.

Want to follow me on social media and see my writing progress? Eager to get peeks of my daily life, and my embarrassingly extensive planner collection? I have you covered.

Follow me here: <u>Facebook</u> - <u>Twitter</u> – <u>Instagram</u> – <u>Website</u>

THE SEVEN SISTERS COTTONWOOD
OMNIBUS EDITION

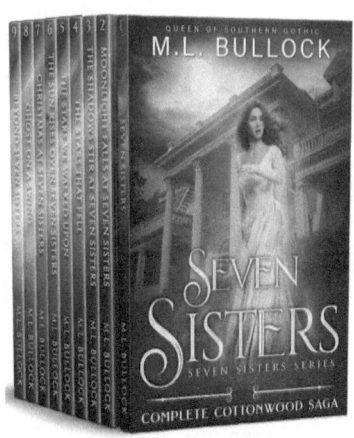

Available now at Amazon and through Kindle Unlimited.

Updated & Expanded FULL Omnibus version for Feb 2020!

The Seven Sisters Ultimate Cottonwood Saga, including two bonus stories.

When historian Carrie Jo Jardine accepted her dream job as the chief historian at Seven Sisters in Mobile, Alabama, she had no idea what she would encounter.

The moldering old plantation housed more than a few boxes of antebellum artifacts and forgotten oil paintings.

Secrets lived there--and they demanded to be set free.

When young, wealthy Ashland Stuart offered Carrie Jo the job, he had no idea that she had a secret of her own.

An unexpected accident takes Carrie Jo back in time as a witness to life at the plantation over 150 years ago.

An impassioned plea from Ashland puts Carrie Jo in a precarious position as the two work together to find young and beautiful missing heiress Calpurnia Cottonwood.

A collection of journals and a series of dreams give Carrie Jo all the clues she needs to find the missing girl, but both a present-day danger and one from the past try to stop her.

Will Carrie Jo solve the mystery of the house *or will she go missing forever herself?*

Grab your copy today!

Author of the best-selling *Seven Sisters* series and the *Gulf Coast Paranormal* series, M.L. Bullock has been storytelling since she was a child. A student of archaeology, she loves weaving stories that feature local Alabama legends. She currently lives on the Gulf Coast with her family but frequently travels to explore the southern states she loves so much. When she's not writing, she enjoys the odd paranormal investigation. The odder, the better.

Connect with M.L. Bullock on Facebook. To receive updates on her latest releases, visit her website at M.L. Bullock and subscribe to her mailing list. You can also contact her at authormlbullock@gmail.com.

OTHER BOOKS BY M.L. BULLOCK

Seven Sisters: The Cottonwood Saga

The Idlewood Collection: The Complete Idlewood Series

Beyond Seven Sisters

The Desert Queen Collection: The Complete Series

The Hauntings of Sugar Hill

Lost Camelot